CORA'S COURAGE

ROMANCE ON THE OREGON TRAIL BOOK ONE

KATHLEEN BALL

This book is dedicated to my husband for all he does

And as always to Bruce, Steven, Colt, Clara and Mavis because I love them

CHAPTER ONE

*S*he cringed and stared at the ground, clasping her hands together and hoping that Eddie would keep his voice down. They'd only been traveling for three weeks with the wagon train, and people avoided her. They were probably all listening to him lecture her on proper behavior.

"Do you think you could act like a proper mother? The only reason Esther cries is because you aren't a good mother."

Cora nodded, not daring to look at him. Bad people came in many disguises and Eddie wore one of the best disguises to cover his badness. Best not to cross him. She smoothed down her serviceable brown skirt and waited for him to stop chiding her. He liked to hear himself talk, she'd concluded. It was best to just let him go on without saying a word in defense. He found fault every day and she never knew what he'd yell at her about.

He went on so long her mind wandered. Everyone already knew that Eddie was always finding fault. She'd had hopes of making a few friends on the trip west but no one wanted to be near them. Not that she blamed them. She walked alone or carried Esther. One friend, just one friend would have meant the world to her, but who would want to get involved with a woman who hung her head in shame daily?

He finished, and she gazed at him, striving for a contrite expression. "I'm sorry, Eddie. I'll do better."

He gave her a quick nod and walked away. It had been the same routine every day for the last three weeks. But unless she wanted another scolding — or worse — she needed to get to her chores. She flew to the back of the wagon, grabbing items she'd need for supper. Without stopping, she pulled the basket Esther napped in close to the back and put down the tailgate to use it as her work table.

She put a cloth sling, she'd made to help carry the baby, across her body and slowly and gently slipped Essie inside. Eddie would have her head if he knew that's what she called her in her mind. Then she grabbed the bucket and started down the steep trail to the fast running creek.

The bank was muddied from the other women who had gotten there before her, making her way quite slippery. She stepped with caution and then finally got on her knees to reach the water. She filled the bucket the best she could and hauled it back to the bank. It would be a hard go making it back up the muddy trail. She wouldn't have cared for herself but now she had her daughter.

She started to slip backwards and felt a hand on her waist and then an arm snaked around her, helping her up the hill. She knew it wasn't Eddie — it would never be Eddie helping her. A peek from beneath her lashes revealed it was Harrison. He often parked his wagon next to theirs. She'd been lectured about that too.

"Thank you, Harrison, but if Eddie sees you helping me..."

"I know, Cora, but how else would you get back up onto the trail?" As soon as she was steadied on her feet, he let go of her and walked away.

The back of her neck prickled, and she slowly turned, her stomach jumping with nerves. Sure enough, Eddie had been watching. Averting her eyes, she hefted the heavy bucket, carried it to their wagon and set it down. Next she took Essie out of the sling and settled her back into her basket.

Eddie never said a word, but his displeasure was easy to read on his face.

"I'll have dinner ready soon."

His eyes narrowed. "See you do."

Her only saving grace was Eddie wasn't a hitting man. And he had been her only choice so she could keep her baby. She'd learn to live through the lectures.

After shredding the leftover grouse meat, she put it in the heavy pot along with water. Then she added a few bits of bacon and chopped carrots. She should have gotten the fire going sooner. She didn't have any kindling to start it. Eddie was right she was a half-wit. Once again she put Essie into the sling and then set out toward the woods.

She wasn't allowed to go into the woods. Scouting the area near the woods didn't yield much, but it was all she could find. Esther was fussing and needed feeding but so did Eddie. For all his words about her not taking good care of Esther, he still expected to come first.

It was slow going carrying both the baby and the kindling, but she hurried the best she could. Her heart sank as she spotted Eddie. His dark hair was always slicked back. She didn't know what he used, but it had an awful smell. He was tall, a bit on the lanky side, and he'd been a nice man when he wanted her for his own. Men always wanted something. Nothing was free; she'd learned that from her mother.

He sat on a crate, brooding as he watched her make the

3

fire and then put the tripod over the flames to hang the pot from. She then had to go into the wagon from the front, which meant climbing up to the bench and then crawling over the seat to the wagon bed. She was only allowed to feed Esther inside the wagon. But feeding her gave her a moment to rest, something she welcomed since she'd been on her feet most of the day.

Usually Eddie wanted her to ride with him in the afternoon, but for some reason today, he had told her to walk. She had fallen behind the rest but then she'd had to feed the baby. It had taken most of her energy to run until she'd caught up. And after feeding the baby, Cora'd had to walk again. And now, her day still held much work.

She finished feeding Esther, burped her, kissed her, and put her back into her basket. Then she climbed out the front and down the side of the wagon. She still had cornbread and dumplings to make. She didn't have milk or an egg for the dumplings but she'd made them with just flour and water before. She finished making the cornbread first and put the dough in her Dutch oven. She set it on some hot coals and shoveled more coals over the top. After that she started on the bread dough. She made bread dough every evening. It rose overnight, and she baked it in the morning.

The weather had been warmer in Independence before they left. Now she wasn't sure it wouldn't snow. It was nice and warm by the fire as she stirred the pot, and when it boiled she dropped the dumplings into the liquid one by one.

Harrison walked by and tipped his hat. "Ma'am, Eddie."

Cora didn't dare acknowledge him. Eddie gave him the barest of nods. It was better that way. If she had said hello, she would have been screamed at for encouraging another man. Eddie always said, "yet another man."

She served Eddie his food and made sure that Eddie had

4

more coffee before she sat down to eat. She'd done so much running around that she had become overheated, and she welcomed the cool air. She had nothing warmer than her shawl but it would have to be enough. In many ways she was grateful to Eddie for helping her.

She ate quickly so she could clean up before dark. She poured water in a pan and washed the dishes and then rinsed them in another tiny amount of water in another pan. She dried everything and put it all away in the spot Eddie had thought best at the beginning of the trip.

It had cost him much money to buy and fill the wagon so they could leave Missouri and he'd done that for her. He must care in his own way.

She fed Esther again and then sat by the fire with Eddie. Her conversation was limited to small observations; the weather, knitting, mending, cooking, or asking his advice on anything. She was not to have any opinions or objections. It was a hard way to live, having to watch every move, every word, and every glance. She was learning not to make him angry.

What type of life would Esther have? Would he constantly lecture the child?

"It's time you went to bed," he told her.

"Of course. Good night." She stood and walked to him to give him a kiss on the cheek. It was another thing he insisted on.

She climbed into the wagon and changed into her flannel nightgown. Then she spread a quilt down on the wooden bottom, lay on it, and used the other half to cover herself with. Eddie slept under the wagon. It was his choice.

Sleep eluded her, and her thoughts drifted to Eddie's obvious displeasure. Maybe if she behaved better, he'd have no reason to lecture her. She sighed. She'd tried that before.

It hadn't been as bad on his farm. There had been no one to hear him but on the wagon train she was so humiliated because he didn't care who heard, and it made the other passengers visibly uncomfortable. She pulled the quilt tighter and prayed she would drift to sleep. She needed her rest. Esther would be up soon and then morning would be here.

She woke up to Esther crying and a strange noise. It sounded like the canvas was being pelted with rocks. The wagon swayed as she quickly snatched up Esther and held her close to protect her.

Eddie jumped into the wagon with his bedroll. "It's hailing and the wind is picking up. He didn't draw the back closed he just stared at the hail.

"Have you ever seen hail so large before?" she asked.

"No."

She turned her back and unbuttoned her gown. Esther didn't seem to mind the hail as long as she was being fed.

"She sure does eat a lot." Eddie commented.

"She has a good appetite."

"She is almost pleasant to look at, but I'm still not giving her my name."

Cora closed her eyes and took a deep breath. "I know."

"I'm not marrying you, either. You're not worthy of the Connor name."

"I understand."

"Do you? Do you really? Tell me why."

Her face heated as she settled Esther back into the basket. "I'm a no good whore who got herself pregnant and was blessed enough to find you."

"That's right. I can leave you behind anytime I like. Remember that."

A flash of lightning probably revealed how red her face was. He'd said nothing about leaving her behind before.

"I'm grateful for all you've done for us, Eddie."

"In what ways would you show me you're grateful?"

It was a trick question. Once she gave him the answer she thought he wanted and was forced to spend the night in a freezing cold barn. She'd been close to her time.

"By obeying you. By being pious and never looking or talking to a man other than you. By making your life easier in any way I can."

"Good." He turned and looked back outside.

He didn't tell her to sleep. Should she? She'd best ask.

"Eddie, may I go back to bed?"

"Yes, you may."

———

HARRISON SHOOK his head in disgust. Where was that woman's spirit? She was so dull with her "yes Eddie, may I Eddie, I'm sorry Eddie." He hated listening to her but no one else wanted to be next to their wagon. He took one side and he didn't know how they decided who took the other.

It was too bad. Cora was so pretty with her fine chestnut color hair and he could have sworn he saw some spunk in her green eyes once but he must have been mistaken. At least Eddie didn't beat her. There had to be a story behind it all, but he sure wasn't privy to it. He stretched as much as he could inside his wagon. It reminded him he wouldn't have much room if his wife, Ora was still alive.

His throat burned every time he thought of her, which was often. It'd had only been six weeks since her death. Going west was something they had planned together. Ora had been so excited to make the trip.

He needed his sleep, but it wasn't happening. He might as well relieve one of the married men from guard duty. He'd survived hail storms before, and he'd do it now.

. . .

THE NEXT DAY the sun came up and the view was spectacular with its pink, blue and purple colors. Harrison still wasn't tired. Lonely yes, tired no. But he'd get through it. He'd never love again, though. His heart still felt as though it had been ripped out.

He was almost to his wagon when he saw Cora balancing on the top of the wooden wagon side with her baby in the sling she used, as she tried to sew closed a hole that had been torn in the canvas. So many watched, but not one person said a word about it being unsafe. Her worthless husband sat by the fire drinking coffee.

She teetered and cried out as she fell hard onto her back.

Harrison ran to her and her eyes were open wide and staring. She looked stunned. Then she turned her head toward him. "Where's Esther?"

He hated the fear in her eyes. "She's right here in her sling." Harrison picked the baby up and showed Cora.

Cora sighed in relief.

"Does anything hurt?" he asked while he handed the baby to one of the women who had come to watch.

"I—I don't know."

"Get away from Cora." Eddie elbowed his way to her and gave Harrison a hard stare. "I'll take care of her." He grabbed the baby away from the woman who held her and glared until the crowd dispersed.

Harrison stepped away from her, but he didn't leave. What was wrong with her husband? Why wasn't he checking his wife for injuries?

Eddie reached a hand down. "Get up."

Cora grabbed his hand and cried out as she tried to stand. "My shoulder and my leg—
"

"Just get up. I know you're fine."

By the time she stood, her face was beyond pale and tears poured down her face.

"You didn't finish the repair."

"I fell."

Eddie stared at her and then at the canvas. He put the baby back in the sling and walked away.

She leaned against the wagon wheel for a moment. Then she took the sling off. Pain flared in her eyes, and she looked ready to cry out, but she clamped her mouth tight. The sling with Esther was gently hung from the wheel as Cora limped to the section where she'd just been. She took a step onto the upside-down wash basin and had trouble getting her other leg to follow. It was a large step onto the side of the wagon, and her body was shaking.

Harrison wanted to carry her down from there, but he couldn't interfere. Eddie would take it out on Cora if he did. It was hard to watch. His gut clenched as she sidestepped to the exact place she needed to be. She grabbed the threaded needle that had been dangling against the canvas and tried to make a stitch but it looked as though she couldn't lift her shoulder. She sidestepped a bit farther and used her left hand to sew. She got two stitches done before she started to tremble again.

"Connor, get your wife down from there!" Captain London yelled. The captain was the leader of the train. People either did things his way, or they got kicked off and had to fend for themselves.

Eddie finished his coffee and then strolled over to where Cora was. "Are you done?"

"No," she mumbled.

"She'll be right down when she's done," Eddie told the captain.

"I want her down now. I heard she already fell once with

the baby. Besides that's not how you repair the canvas. You need to take it off to darn it and then patch it. You can't just sew it. Water will get in."

Eddie gave the captain an insolent glance. "You heard him," he snapped at Cora. "Get down offa there."

Cora was on one foot while leaning her body against one rib of the wagon. Her eyes were closed, and Harrison suspected she couldn't get herself down.

He'd had enough. He walked to her and gently talked her into trusting him to lift her down. After a time, she nodded. "We'll need a doctor," he told the captain.

"Drop down so I can grab your waist." He lifted her down but kept her in his arms.

Mrs. Chapman came running. "Harrison set her on the tailgate so I can look her over. I might need her moved inside the wagon. Where's the baby? Mr. Connor do you have the baby?"

Captain London picked up the sling from the wagon wheel. "The baby is right here."

"Harrison, bring her to my wagon. Captain, same with the baby." Eddie stood up. Mrs. Chapman held up her hand. "I don't want to hear it, Mr. Connor. I'll let you know when you can come get them." She led the procession to her wagon while she mumbled and shook her head.

Harrison glanced down at Cora. "I guess there's been a change in plans."

"No! Put me down and give me Esther. The only wagon I'm going to is mine. Where is Eddie?" Her eyes were wide and her voice wavered.

"You need not be scared," Harrison said in a soft voice.

"You don't understand. If he thinks I left... Please take me back." Her eyes filled with tears. "Please."

Both Mrs. Chapman and the captain stopped. Mrs.

Chapman turned them around and headed back to the Connor wagon.

Harrison set her down on the tailgate and Esther was placed in the basket. Eddie glared at him.

CHAPTER TWO

*A*s soon as everyone left, Cora fed Esther and waited in dread for Eddie to come see her. She didn't dare move from the wagon until he told her what to do. He'd been humiliated and he would not take it quietly.

It seemed like hours before he appeared. She couldn't help the tears that fell.

"I'm sorry that I was so clumsy. It's my fault. Then I didn't know what to do with all those people around. I'm used to it being just you and me and now Esther. I didn't like the way Mrs. Chapman talked either."

Some of the fury in his eyes died down. "Everything happened so fast."

"I know, and I'm sorry. I didn't know to use a patch. I deserve your anger."

"You did the right thing insisting to be brought back here."

She heard someone clear his voice outside and had the feeling it was Harrison. Eddie didn't act as though he heard it.

"People will put their noses in our business for the next

13

few days. You're to stay in the wagon, no excuses. I'm sure one of the women will bring meals over. Then it'll be back to work."

"Yes, Eddie." She kept her gaze down until he left. She couldn't do this anymore. It was no way to live. She smiled at Esther and sighed. It was the only way for her to have her baby. She'd have to endure it. Men like Harrison thought her to be a weak ninny, but she didn't have a choice.

She'd had few choices in her life until she was eleven years old. Then she was sold and from then on, they had told her what to do, wear, and think. Her rebellious streak had never died, though. But now she might have to let it die and become the woman Eddie wanted her to be. People from her past might still be looking for her, but hopefully they thought her long gone or dead.

Eddie had seemed like a different man when he'd offered to help her. He'd acted sane, but as soon as he had her hidden at his house he began to tell her what to think, wear, and do. At least she had Esther, though. She'd do what she had to for her daughter.

It had been four days, and Cora hadn't even poked her head out of the wagon. Her entire body ached from being jostled and bumped while riding in it. If she hadn't known better, she would have thought Eddie was deliberately hitting each rut on the ground. Her leg still hurt, but the rest of her was fine. She'd be able to do her work.

They stopped for the noon meal, and she called Eddie's name.

He went right to her. He must think he had cowed her even more than she already had been and was lapping it all up.

"I—as long as you agree that is—I'd like to get back to

doing my work. I don't want you to have to work any harder than you already are."

He smiled a knowing smile, a triumphant smile, and she wanted to throw up.

"Yes, you may get out of the wagon and work. It has been trying for me." He walked away.

Trying? Women she didn't even know brought them meals. He hadn't lifted a finger. She found that taking deep breaths helped her stay calm. She'd made her choice a year ago, and it was hers to live with.

She was putting her unruly hair up properly when she heard Harrison talking.

"She's a meek mouse. I'm not sure she has a single thought of her own in her brain. I felt sorry for her at first, but now, I can hardly abide looking at her. She needs no one to help her. She has her husband."

Cora stilled, and her stomach churned.

She'd thought highly of Harrison but not anymore. It was his right to think what he liked, but to talk about her? She listened for a response but they must have moved away from the side of the wagon.

Why his words could hurt her so, she did not understand. But they cut deeper than they should have. She made sure Esther was fine in her basket before she climbed out of the wagon.

Usually for the nooning most ate what they'd had for breakfast. There wasn't time to build fires and make a meal. She saw they had biscuits and bacon and felt relieved.

"I'd like hot coffee. You must find some wood."

She nodded to Eddie and began to walk.

"Don't forget Esther."

Her face heated. "Thank you for reminding me." She climbed back in and found the sling. Gently put Essie into it. She was a beautiful child. She looked a lot like her father. She got them out of the wagon and walked toward the woods. Eddie always assumed she didn't know who the father was just as he assumed she was a whore. Granted she'd lived in a whore house—she had since she was eleven, but she was never paid to… she was never paid. They thought her to be ten and too young.

There had been a boy, Rudy, who came by every day to use the piano. It took a year for him to talk to her and another four before he proposed. No one had taught her about what proper women did. No one told her she had to wait until she was married. He had told her being engaged was enough.

It had only been once, and she loved him with all her heart, and she knew he loved her back. It wasn't until she was sick in the mornings that Madam Grealy took her aside and asked her about it.

How could she have lived in a whore house and be so naïve? Madam Grealy was furious and told the bartender, Bosley to get rid of Rudy and the baby. Someone stabbed Rudy that same day, and the next day Bosley had told Cora they had to go somewhere. The other girls had already told her how her life would be after that.

One girl, Macey, helped her to escape by asking Eddie to get Cora out of town. She'd been with him ever since.

Glancing around, all she saw were trees. She wasn't supposed to go into the woods. She quickly grabbed some fallen branches as she panicked. As she scurried to the edge of the woods, she ran into Harrison.

"Your husband is looking for you."

The blood drained from her face, leaving her somewhat lightheaded, and she ran back to the wagon. Her heart pounded. Somehow she knew this would send Eddie over the edge.

Eddie took the wood from her and threw it on the ground. "Get in that wagon. Now!"

She hurried and got into the wagon as fast as she could. He followed her.

"I'd love to take a belt to you, but I don't want to leave scars. I thought about taking Esther from you, but the others on the train wouldn't like it. I've decided that you are to only get two spoonfuls of corn mush a day. An empty stomach should teach you to obey me."

"I'm sorry, Eddie. I will do as you say."

"You'll walk for the rest of the day and do all your chores tonight, but no dinner."

"Yes, Eddie."

"Looks as though we are moving out. Don't fall behind."

"What do I do when Esther is hungry?"

"Feed her while you walk. Let everyone see how shameful you really are."

She swallowed hard and nodded. Out of the corner of her eye she saw Harrison pass her. He was probably laughing at her for being a mouse without a brain.

Cora should have brought her shawl and put on woolen stockings but she didn't have that chance. The cold wind blew, and she was cold to her bones. The other women didn't walk with her. And when she fed Esther, it made her all the colder. Eddie was right; it felt shameful to have men watch. Other women always had a way to cover themselves. She covered herself the first feeding with the sling but Eddie told her she wasn't to do it that way. Too bad she wasn't a meek mouse; she'd just lie down and die.

The temperature continued to drop. Her feet turned numb, but her main concern was to keep Esther as warm as possible. Eddie used to care what happened to Esther.

Wagon after wagon passed her by as she tried to keep from stumbling. One wagon pulled out of line and halted. It was Harrison's, but she couldn't stop, didn't dare even acknowledge him.

"Cora, you must be frozen. Think about the baby."

"Eddie said it must be this way. I went into the woods, and I've caused him a lot of trouble lately. I have to go."

"Take a blanket! It's getting colder by the minute."

She looked longingly at the warm blanket but shook her head. "I'm not allowed." As she kept walking, she heard him curse.

She stepped as fast as she dared, trying to keep warm. The ruts were deep and slippery, and she fell to her knees too many times to count, but she got back up and kept going. Her leg hadn't completely healed, but she tried to put the pain out of her mind.

Esther woke and needed to be nursed. Cora wrapped her in the sling and then openly nursed her. It didn't much matter as long as Esther was fed. She was almost done when she saw that Harrison's wagon had stopped again.

"Cora, let me at least take the baby. She'll die out here."

Snow had begun to fall, and Cora nodded. She held Esther up to Harrison.

"She's like ice!"

"I know." Her tears wouldn't stop falling as she walked away without looking back at her child.

CHAPTER THREE

he sun was setting, and they kept going. It was torture. As far as she could tell, she was the only walker. Snow was coming down heavily now. Her fingers were turning purple, and she hadn't felt her feet in hours. They'd be stopping soon. What would she make for Eddie to eat? She was glad she had put the wood he'd thrown on the ground in the back of the wagon.

She had salt pork, and she could make corncakes. He'd have many meals out of the one. She needed to walk faster. If they stopped and she took too long to catch up… The pain in her leg disappeared. In fact, she didn't feel her legs at all. It made for difficult walking, but she continued.

They were circling the wagons when Captain London rode her way. "Come on, Give me your hand."

"I'm supposed to walk."

"I'm in charge here. Give me your hand."

She held out her hand to the big, older man and felt herself lifted onto the horse to sit in front of the captain.

"You're colder than ice. Where's your warmer clothes? Where's the baby?"

"Harrison has Esther. She was getting too cold and he offered."

"He didn't offer you a ride too?"

"Eddie said I had to walk. I went into the woods during the nooning, and I wasn't supposed to."

"That's no excuse. He should have pulled off and taken you into the wagon. All you have on is a dress. Another mile and you'd be dead. He knew the baby was out here?" His voice sounded deadly.

"Yes," she whispered.

He opened his coat and drew her against him. "Hold the ends closed if you can." He slowed down. "Hold still. Your hands won't work, will they?" He shifted her closer and buttoned his coat around both of them.

Captain London spurred his palomino on. They were the last to reach the camp. The captain rode right past Eddie and stopped at Harrison's wagon. He already had a fire blazing warming a blanket and a couple warming irons.

Once the captain unbuttoned his coat, Harrison took her from the horse and set her on a crate near the fire. He put the blanket on her and turned to his wagon, returning a few moments later with wool socks.

Captain London was already kneeling next to her taking her shoes off. "Quick, heat some water so we can soak her feet!"

"No! That makes it worse," Mrs. Chapman said as she ran toward them. "Apply cold water, then cool water, then warm water. We'll need cloths. Where is Esther?"

"She's sleeping in my wagon," Harrison told her. "She's all warmed up and asleep."

"Where is Mr. Connor? Has he no care for his wife and child?"

"He sought to punish her by making her walk all day," Harrison explained.

"He ought to be horsewhipped," Captain London said.

What had started as the pricks of hundreds of needles in her feet was quickly turning to searing agony. "It hurts," Cora cried.

The next thing she knew everyone was surrounding her with homemade cures. Mrs. Chapman had someone make willow bark tea and she took a bottle of brandy another traveler handed her.

The pain was worse than anything she'd felt before. She wanted to lie down in the wagon.

Eddie appeared with a trunk and set it down with a hard *thunk* next to Cora. "Here are all her things. Someone else can take responsibility for her now. I'm done."

Cora closed her eyes. She couldn't take much more.

"You can't kick your family out!" Captain London yelled.

"We're not married and that is not my kid. I rescued her from a whore house. I was doing her a favor, and this is what I get? I want nothing to do with her. Harrison if you're so worried about her, you can keep her." Eddie stomped off.

Cora opened her eyes. It was suddenly so quiet she could hear the snowflakes hitting the packed snow on the ground. They had all condemned her.

"I'm sorry."

———

HARRISON PICKED HER UP. "I'll need warm blankets. If you're not here to help go back to your wagons and do your gossiping," he announced. He handed her to the captain and climbed in his wagon. He put one warm blanket down on his mattress tick and then he took her from the captain. As gently as he could, he placed her on it and covered her with another blanket.

Someone handed him the wrapped warming irons, and

he placed them between the blankets. He could see the pain on her face as she tried to bite her lip probably to keep from crying out. Perhaps she wasn't a mouse maybe she was actually brave.

He and Mrs. Chapman spent most of the night tending to Cora. In between he'd leave the wagon so Cora could feed Esther with Mrs. Chapman's help.

He sat on a crate and stared at the fire. What was he supposed to do with Cora and the baby? Not married? She'd been a whore with child when Eddie helped her? He knew what everyone else thought. He'd heard it all night, but he wasn't sure what he thought.

Right now, he had but one concern. Which family would take her in?

He hated hearing her cries of pain but laudanum and morphine were bad for a nursing baby. Most people left and went to their own wagons. What if no one offered to take her? Minister Paul and his wife Della promised to bring them all supper. Harrison felt as though he couldn't breathe and the world was closing in on him. He didn't mind helping Cora get better, but he couldn't take her in his wagon. How would it look?

He sighed, for her reputation was beyond that now, but he didn't want his name besmirched. The minister and his wife would be obligated wouldn't they? There had to be someone. They wouldn't leave her behind.

He carried the reheated warming irons and gave them to Mrs. Chapman. "How is she?"

"She's lucky. There isn't any permanent damage, but her fingers and toes pain her something awful. I can't believe what Mr. Connor said about her. She has conducted herself with the greatest of virtue. I'll wait to hear what she has to say before I decide. She'd had to have been the loneliest person traveling. Not one woman walked with her and her husband — er, I mean Mr. Connor made it impossible to visit their fire. It must be hard with a small baby. It's a time you want women to give you advice and reassure you you're doing everything right. But If Mr. Connor hadn't rescued her; I don't think Esther would have been born. You don't hear too many stories about soiled doves with children."

He rubbed the back of his neck. "I suppose you're right. I'm hoping the minister and his wife will take her."

Mrs. Chapman smiled and took the heating irons to place under the blankets.

A cloud passed over the full moon, and for a moment all was dark. He'd bet Cora's life had a lot of darkness in it.

"Here, I have bread and salt pork with beans. I'm glad I put extra beans to soak last night. There is plenty so eat up. I'll make a plate for Mrs. Chapman," Della said. She put the heavy pot and a loaf of bread on a barrel outside the wagon.

"I appreciate it. Thank you."

Minister Paul sat down next to Harrison. "You're not married, are you?"

"No."

"Promised to anyone?"

Harrison narrowed his eyes. "Why?"

"I asked around and no one will take them in. Our wagon is full of Bibles, and there isn't room. Captain London has it in his head you can marry Cora." The minister stared at him as though trying to gauge his reaction.

Harrison's first instinct was to run. He would not be hog-tied to Cora. Now that he knew what she was, he didn't want to look at her. It might not be her fault but he couldn't help the way he felt.

"That won't work for me. The captain can find another fool to marry that… that… Cora." His face heated. He'd almost called her a whore.

The minister nodded. "You might as well eat."

CORA STIFFENED at Harrison's words. It hurt, but he was just speaking the truth as he saw it. What would happen to her and Essie? Not one person wanted her. No one offered to take her and Essie in. It wouldn't matter so much but what about Essie? Maybe she could find someone to take her to raise as their own. If they left just her behind, her mind would be at ease, knowing her daughter was safe.

"Mrs. Chapman. I need to speak with Harrison please."

Mrs. Chapman stared at her for a moment and then nodded. Mrs. Chapman climbed out of the wagon and Harrison climbed in. The look on his face said it all. He didn't want to talk to her.

She shifted. Spikes of sheer torture shot up her legs, and she ended up crying out. She waited until it passed before she gazed at Harrison. "I need you to find a family for Essie. A forever family. Good people."

"You want to give away your baby?" The look in his eyes was anything but kind.

"I'll stay behind. I want Essie safe." Tears spilled down her face. "Please."

His Adam's apple bobbed as he swallowed, and then he nodded and said, "Yes."

She relaxed. His word could be trusted. He was a good man. She studied his strong chin and high cheek bones. His dark hair could have used a trim. His eyes were a soft gray color, and his lips were usually upturned at the corners but not tonight. He stared back at her until she turned her head away.

Shame flooded her, and accompanied by the intense pain, it was all unbearable. Just drawing her next breath over-whelmed her. A series of decisions had made it so she was now unacceptable. Most decisions hadn't even been hers—

except for Rudy. Her heart cried out for him, but he was dead. A solitary tear rolled over her cheek. As long as Essie would be cared for, she could take whatever the future held.

"CORA, WAKE UP, DEAR," Mrs. Chapman urged.

Cora opened her eyes and the pain screamed through her. "Essie?"

"Harrison would like to talk to you. Here drink this." She put a cup to Cora's mouth and poured the contents into her mouth. Cora almost spit it out. It was liquor. She shuddered.

"It's just a small amount, and it should help with the pain."

Cora watched Mrs. Chapman climb out the back again. A moment later, Harrison climbed in. He made the wagon seem so much smaller. She held her breath. Was it time to say good bye to Essie?

"Who is taking her?"

He shook his head. "A few offered, but I didn't deem them to be of good character. One was a single man. He only offered for her, not the two of you, and I didn't like that. Another has a passel of kids that looked as though they hadn't had a good meal in months. I couldn't bring myself to leave her with them."

Her heart dropped. "Thank you anyway. We'll get by somehow if someone will leave me some supplies when you all ride off tomorrow. I'm not afraid. I'm a firm believer that when one door closes another opens. Your kindness has meant the world to me. Could you put Essie lying with her head on my shoulder? My hands hardly work, but I need her close."

He picked up the little one from the basket, and she appeared even smaller in his big hands. He gently laid the baby down and made sure she was in a good position to keep from slipping off.

"I understand people hating me, but a little baby? She is innocent."

He cleared his throat. "I think people thought someone else would take her. I failed you, and I'm sorry."

"You look so tired and I'm lying on your tick mattress. I bet you'll be relieved when I'm gone. Eddie wasn't the nicest man, but he provided for us. I tried to be everything he wanted so this wouldn't happen."

Mrs. Chapman poked her head in. "I'll get some sleep and check on you in the morning."

"Thank you for your kindness."

"My dear, it's my pleasure."

When she was gone, Cora's stomach churned. There went her one ally. Well, perhaps not an ally, but she was kind.

Essie began to cry and there was a hint of panic in Harrison's eyes.

"If you can just take her for a moment, I can bring her under the blanket and feed her."

"Are you sure?"

"Pain doesn't matter when it comes to Essie. I can do it."

He held the baby and helped to put her under the blanket into Cora's arms. Cora's face heated as Harrison saw her bare shoulder, but there was no help for it.

He turned and watched out the back of the wagon while Essie nursed.

HE HAD PLANNED to get some sleep under the wagon but he couldn't leave Cora and Essie alone. What if the baby needed to be fed again?

He shook his head in amazement. How was this all taking place in his wagon? He should have minded his own business. No, that wouldn't have been the right thing.

What would Ora have done? He smiled. She would have made sure that Cora never walked alone in the first place. She would have taken them in. He could offer his protection, but he had a bad feeling it would mean marriage. He was still hurting from Ora's death. He squared his shoulders. As long as Cora didn't touch him, he might do it. Discouragement rolled over him. There were twenty-six wagons in the group, and he was the only one willing to take responsibility for a fellow passenger?

Ora, you're still in my heart. I'm just helping this woman and her baby. I don't particularly like the woman, but I can't allow her to be left behind. It's a death sentence. It's unseemly for me to marry so soon but I'm hoping you'll be with me on this decision. I miss you every minute of every day. I often think you're still here but when I want to show you something or talk to you I realize you are gone, my love.

He leaned against the closed tailgate and fell asleep.

"Cora, let me comb your hair for your wedding," Mrs. Chapman said as she kneeled next to her.

"What wedding? Who's getting married? Will they be able to give Essie a home?" Her thoughts were so jumbled. "Where is Essie?" She tried to sit up but Mrs. Chapman held her shoulder down.

"She's been fed and now she's napping."

"How? I was sleeping."

"I know. I tried to wake you but Essie knew what to do. No one else saw a thing I kept you covered. Now I need to comb your hair before Minister Paul tells me to get out of the wagon. It's for the best, dear."

Mrs. Chapman finished braiding her hair, so it hung down on one side, and then she hurried out of the wagon.

She must be dreaming. *Everything is too fuzzy in my mind.* How could she not awaken to feed her baby? It made little sense.

Harrison climbed into the wagon looking freshly washed and shaved. Minister Paul followed him.

She was so tired she wanted to just close her eyes. "What?"

"Everything will be fine, Cora," Harrison said.

Was the minister performing a wedding? She said something to him and closed her eyes.

Wait! Who kissed her forehead?

Three hours later, Cora sat up. She was in a moving wagon. Her heart slowed from its panicked rate when she saw Essie in a basket. They'd probably leave them behind when they stopped for the nooning. Someone must have given her something; she'd never slept this long. Was it the brandy? She wouldn't think it would have such an effect on her.

She reached for Essie, and her body exploded in pain that took her breath away. She waited a minute before she lifted Essie out of the basket. The baby opened her eyes and waved her hands. Cora let the blanket slip down and easily fed the eager baby. Cora sent up thanks and praise for her small reprieve.

Using her fingers hurt. But she held Essie to her and burped her. They said if they gave her anything to ease the pain it would affect Essie. Well, she seemed just fine. Cora hummed as she rocked her baby, and when she finished humming, she remembered someone had gotten married. Was it last night? She thought and thought on it, and the pieces came together.

Oh, my!

She was the one who'd gotten married. Did she marry Harrison?

She was in his wagon. The poor man had sacrificed to keep them from being left behind. A tear rolled down her cheek. It wasn't fair to him to be saddled with her. When they stopped, she'd give him his freedom.

She heard the calling for the noon time stop. Her body shook in fear. She tried to stop its trembling, but she had no control over it. She carefully put Essie in her bed and then lay back down, trying to pull the blanket up. She couldn't raise it enough to cover her shoulders, and a wave of shame washed over her.

Harrison climbed in as soon as the wagon stopped and surveyed her. Tears gathered in her eyes at his inspection.

"Could you pull the blanket up to cover me completely? I fed Essie, but I couldn't get the blanket any higher. I'm sorry. I tried, but my fingers didn't want to."

He shifted the blanket, so she was covered and fixed the other blankets covering her. "I know you're in pain. You're shaking, are you still cold?"

"I'm terrified. Someone must have dosed me with something. I didn't wake up for a feeding and it took me forever to figure out it was us that got married. My head was so fuzzy. You need not take me in. It's not fair to you. I'm sure you have other plans for your life and I'll not have you ruin it by having me as your wife."

He smiled. "I never figured you for a woman who gave an opinion. You always did what you were told."

Dismay filled her. She would never have thought Harrison to be like Eddie. Perhaps many men wanted quiet obedient women. She had no experience except for Rudy, and he'd always asked what she thought.

"I'm sorry. I won't question you again." She turned her head. She knew nothing of being a married woman.

Mrs. Chapman poked her head in again. "Do you need my help with anything?"

"Yes, please," Cora said hoping she wasn't making Harrison angry.

He touched her cheek until she turned and gazed at him. "We'll talk later. I think you'll find I'm nothing like Eddie."

She tried to smile, but she failed.

CHAPTER FOUR

he last week hadn't been easy. Helping Cora brought a longing he needed to get rid of. He sighed. At least she could do things for herself now. Helping her to dress was too much for him. She was beautiful, but he made good and sure his touch didn't linger. Now he wouldn't have to worry about putting her stockings on.

Every time they'd stopped he carried her outside to sit for a while. The fresh air was good for her. The others staring at her wasn't. She had done nothing untoward to deserve their censure. She was a kind young woman who was very loving to her daughter. She'd relaxed a bit when he explained he didn't want a meek wife. She still tried to please him by keeping everything exactly where he had put it. She always agreed with him. Other than that she'd been quiet.

He made a fire and put the coffee on to boil while she dressed herself and Essie. He smiled and stood when she waited at the back of the wagon with the basket in her hands. He reached up and took the basket.

"Stay where you are. I don't want you to climb down." He

hated her nod. All it meant was she'd do as he said. He wasn't used to biddable women. Ora certainly had ideas of her own.

After setting the basket down, he reached up and put his hands on her waist while she put her hands on his shoulders. He lifted her down easily. He wanted to be close to her for just a moment but stopped himself.

"It's nice to see you up and around," he told her.

"It took quite a while didn't it? Thank you for all your help." She blushed and glanced away.

Was she trying to entice him? She acted unknowing and innocent but she wasn't. She couldn't be. Was it all an act she had perfected?

HE GREASED the wheels and watched as she cooked breakfast. He just didn't know what to make of her. Her actions weren't anything like he would expect, given her past. How long had she been a whore? He turned away. He shouldn't think of his wife that way. He wanted to ask, but he wanted the truth, not what she thought he wanted her to say.

They ate bacon, biscuits, and corn mush. It was better than what he'd been cooking. She had watched as he took each bite and dismay had his stomach in a knot. How could one live in constant fear of displeasing another? He needed to talk to her and soon.

Little Essie had stolen his heart. One look into her blue eyes, and he was smitten. He had held her plenty these last weeks, and she always stared at him with a look of wonder. He hoped that look never went away.

"I must do laundry soon. Essie's diapers leak at night, and her blankets get soaked. I need to freshen them. Also, I'm sure you have clothes that need washing?"

"I think we're stopping early today near water for just that reason."

She smiled. "It's been wonderfully warmer. I didn't expect snow early in the trip."

"It caught me off guard too, but from what I've learned it's not uncommon. It's hard to judge when to leave Independence. If you go too early, you'll encounter more snow than we did. If you leave late you take the chance of not being able to get through the mountain pass due to snow."

"I'm grateful for the warmth of the sun this morning. Shall I walk today?"

"Not today. You're still a bit weak. I want you where I can see you."

She nodded and quickly glanced away.

"I'm not like Eddie, Cora. I don't want to control everything you do, but you have been flat on your back for a week. If you're up for it after the noon meal, we can talk about it again." She stared at him and her eyes widened. Hadn't she been given choices before or had Eddie soured her on all men?

"My mother used to paint some diapers with linseed oil to waterproof the outside for nighttime. She'd put it over the first diaper to double up. Maybe we can do that when we get those diapers washed. They need to be dry."

She tilted her head. "You have much knowledge, and I thank you for sharing it with me. I was sold to Madam Grealy when I was eleven and I can read and write and do some adding and such but they didn't think I'd need school. It took me a long time to realize why."

"Sold?"

"Yes. I'd been at the orphanage for a few months before I was taken to the saloon. I washed sheets and the women's clothing. I cleaned the saloon too in the morning when the customers were gone. I didn't understand what was going on or what plans they had for me. I'm glad I never found out." She gathered the dishes and washed them.

It would be wonderful if he could believe her, but the proof of her lies was sleeping in the basket. It hurt that she didn't trust him, but perhaps in time. "I will check on the livestock."

"Do you have more than the oxen?"

"I have a string of horses and almost thirty head of cattle too. I pay three men to help me out. Don't be surprised if they stop by for meals. It was part of the deal but they didn't like my cooking so much."

She nodded and went back to washing the dishes. How long would it take until she trusted him? They had four to five months on the trail to find out.

CORA FROWNED. She'd expected at least one question about her life at the saloon. It was strange. Maybe he didn't care. She'd been thrust on him and he was under no obligation to like her. He sure liked Essie though. He'd be a good father someday. She'd call him a good father now, but she had no idea what would happen at the end of the trail. Men had left wives before. Harrison was a good man but she couldn't hide her background. Everyone already knew.

She put Essie in the wagon and then climbed in the front. Harrison climbed up.

"I would have helped you up. Husbands do that for their wives."

Her face heated. "I'll know for next time." She pretended to be interested in something on her side of the wagon.

"I've embarrassed you."

"No, I'm inadequate. I know little about how things are done. My father was a gruff man who said nothing kind. People avoided us. I learned to be respectful in school. The concept of sharing was hard to grasp. But my teacher was understanding and took the time to teach me a few manners. I'll always be grateful to her."

"Wagons Ho!" Came the call.

Soon it was their turn. "Hold on to the seat."

He was so different from Eddie, who had laughed and laughed when she fell off one day.

They rode for a few hours and then they forded another river. Each crossing scared her more than the one before.

"We're not stopping here to use river water for washing and drinking?" She furrowed her brow.

"There's a creek up ahead that has more grass for the livestock. We'll stop there."

"I'm looking forward to it."

Then Essie cried, and Cora climbed into the back with Harrison holding on to her. He made her feel as though she was a woman of value.

After feeding Essie, she lay down for just a moment and woke when the wagon stopped. She quickly sat up and crawled behind the front bench. "I'm so sorry. I didn't mean to fall asleep."

After tying off the lines, he turned and looked at her. "There is no reason to be sorry. There wasn't anything else that needed doing. There isn't much that can be done while the wagon sways and bumps along."

She blinked at him. Was he extra nice? Or had Eddie been extra cruel? Probably both.

"We drove through the nooning. I'll get the food out while you gather the laundry."

"I should do both. What will the other women think?"

He climbed into the back with her and kneeled facing her. He put his thumb under her chin and tilted her head until she saw his eyes. They looked kind, concerned even.

"You are my wife, and anyone who mistreats you will have to answer to me. The key is we need to act as a happy couple. Smiling at each other, holding hands and me kissing you on the cheek will make them think I feel that I've made a good choice." His expression softened into a smile. "Being married is about learning what the other is like, what things in the world they are interested in. Their likes and dislikes. It's about trying things and working out the problems. We'll be fine."

"You sound as though you've been married before."

He acted as though she'd punched him in the stomach. Face contorted in obvious pain, he climbed out of the wagon and walked away.

Cora stared after him. What had just happened? A frown pinched her forehead. Maybe Eddie was right and she couldn't do anything right. It saddened her more than she ever expected. Eddie wasn't a good man, and Harrison is too good.

She gathered the laundry and then put Essie in the sling. She grabbed some soap and carried it all in the basket she'd been using for Essie's bed. After pushing everything toward the tailgate she put it down. She lifted Essie and put the sling across her body. It was awkward carrying the basket with the sling, but she managed.

There wasn't anyone else at the creek yet. They were all probably eating. She kneeled on the bank and started scrubbing the clothes. She put the wet things back in the basket intending to wring the water from them all next. She was just finishing up when she heard others come down to the bank.

Next, she was pushed and someone said, "Oops." All of Cora's wash was dumped in the creek.

She didn't bother to look at any of the women. She walked into the creek with Essie. The clothes that remained on the surface, she grabbed and threw them on the bank. How was she going to get the clothing and blankets that had sunk? The creek wasn't too fast moving and she was grateful.

She couldn't bend down to search for anything without Essie getting dunked in the water. She had no one to ask to hold Essie. Her heart sank. It was one thing after another and for a moment she thought she'd break.

"Cora!" Mrs. Chapman called. "I'll hold the baby for you."

Cora nodded and waded to the bank. "Thank you," she said as she handed Essie to the woman.

Cora took the basket with her. Time after time she bent and felt around for the precious clothing. She gathered the blankets and most of Harrison's garments. Her own things were becoming elusive. Diapers she could ill afford to lose were gone. Again, she waded to the creek's edge and put the wet things on the now muddy bank. She waded downstream, hunting for her things. Her eyes welled with tears but she ruthlessly blinked them back. She didn't want whoever did this to see her cry. She found a few diapers and kept going, looking for her clothes. Soon she couldn't see the bank or the women. She found a few underthings and stockings. A diaper was hanging on a rock ahead, and she sloshed forward.

She was beyond exhausted, but she had to have clothes to wear. She recovered one dress and decided to go back. It was harder walking in the other direction. The water was cold. She'd been so intent on finding their things she didn't give it much thought. The dress she wore weighed heavily on her, and she had to stop and rest. All was fairly peaceful until she heard Harrison yell at the women.

Cora knew then she'd be just fine. She took a few more weighted steps before he was there. His arms were outstretched and she'd never seen a better sight.

"How far did you go?" He clasped her to him.

"See the big rock in front of the tree? A diaper was there.

And beyond that I found one of my dresses. I would have looked for more but my strength was waning. Essie is fine, isn't she?"

He took the basket from her. "Yes, our daughter is just fine."

Joy filled her. *Our* daughter. "Thank you."

"What happened?"

"I was just about done washing. I was alone then a bunch of women came and I heard what sounded like one tripped. I was jostled and my clothes all ended up in the water. You'd think they'd know how precious each item of clothing is. Some don't have as much as others. I'm glad you came looking for us."

With his arm around her waist he helped her along until they got to the bank.

"Stay right here. I'll lift you out." He placed the basket on the bank and then turned back to her. He scooped her up. "Your dress weighs a ton, and you're shivering." He sat her on the bank and then climbed out.

"Mrs. Chapman, could you be so kind as to bring Essie to our fire? I'm afraid my wife may end up sick. She's shaking, and I need to get her by the fire. I will be back for the clothes, and if any are missing your husbands or fathers will hear about it."

She closed her eyes. She couldn't bear to see the way people were probably staring at her.

"Some people can't do anything right."

It was Eddie's voice and it was the last straw. All the fight left Cora, and she sagged in Harrison's arms. She didn't deserve everyone's disdain.

He set her inside the wagon. "Throw your wet things out here."

Good, he tightened the canvas so no one could look inside at her. She hesitated about throwing her underclothes out to him but then remembered he'd been married before.

She shook her head. So far, it had been an all-around bad day.

HARRISON PUT another log on the fire. They probably thought it to be a funny trick, but it was mean. How old was she? He had judged her to be about eighteen, but with her hair all wet and pushed away from her face she looked younger.

"I have the wet things." Her subdued voice came from the wagon.

He loosened the rope that held the canvas closed, and his jaw dropped. His heart pounded as he looked away.

"I have nothing to wear, and the blankets are wet. My shawl is with Eddie, I guess."

He took the wet clothes and closed the back again. "I'll find something for you."

He took a deep breath. She'd been curled up so he couldn't see much. But it had been enough. Somehow, she was drawing him to her and he wasn't ready.

He asked the minister's wife if she had an extra nightgown. Della was very gracious and gave him one that practically looked new. Then he hurried back to the wagon and reached inside, the gown in his hand but without having to look.

"I'm going to see about Essie, our clothes, and your shawl. There are extra wool socks in my trunk you can wear."

He met Mrs. Chapman on the way to the creek. She took his hand and gave it a gentle squeeze. "I'll stay until you get back. No rush."

He nodded. What would they do without her? There were

still several women at the creek. Someone had rinsed their clothes and wrung them. He spied two unwed young women holding up Cora's garments against them, laughing and saying how ugly the dresses were.

He snatched the dresses away and didn't say a word. He bent and picked up the basket.

"Such a waste to marry someone like her."

He put the basket back down and gazed at the group of women. He didn't know who'd spoken, so he addressed them all. "She's chilled through. She just got over what Mr. Connor did to her by making her walk in the snow. It wasn't a fun prank, it's dangerous for her. I don't care what gossip you've listened to, but I have found her to be a good woman and a wonderful mother." He picked up the basket and started to leave.

"What about a good wife? She's bound to be excellent in that way too."

If they were men, he'd have taken a swing. He kept walking he still had to collect the shawl. When he asked Eddie about it he denied knowing anything about a shawl. Harrison practically growled at Eddie and the shawl was quickly found.

He slowed down for a moment and took a few deep breaths. He didn't want Cora to think he was mad at her. He could thank Eddie for that too.

He smiled when he saw her. She had two pairs of his socks on, and someone had given her a quilt to drape around her. She almost took his breath away, sitting there by the fire.

He couldn't resist getting closer and kissing her cheek. The smile she gave him was worth it.

"I'll get a couple lines set up to hang the clothes."

"At least have a cup of coffee or a biscuit first."

"We'll be losing daylight soon. It won't take but a minute." He used the poles that held up his tent to attach the ropes to.

One end was tied to the wagon, so he had two lines which he hoped would keep others from staring.

"You found my dresses!" Her voice quavered.

"Yes, sweet, I did and someone rinsed and wrung the clothes."

She nodded and looked like she wanted to sob. As quick as he could, he got the clothes hung and then sliced bacon to cook to have with the biscuits. They ate in silence.

"Thank you for all you did today. I'd probably still be in the creek if you hadn't come."

He stood and picked her up. He set her down on his lap and held her. She sobbed as he rubbed her back. When she finished, he rocked her back and forth. She wasn't shaking and it relieved him.

Essie began to fuss. He gave Cora a big hug and released her. She stood, and he lifted her into the wagon. Hopefully she'd go to sleep.

He stared into the fire and realized he didn't have a place to bed down for the night. His tent poles were in use, and all the blankets were wet. He'd have to tell her not to wash everything at once next time.

"Evening, Harrison," Captain London greeted. He took a deep draw from his pipe. "I heard you had a spot of trouble."

"Nothing that couldn't be taken care of."

The captain sat down. "You've taken a lot on, and I thank you. I didn't know what I would do."

Harrison lowered his voice. "How old do you think she is?"

"Seventeen? I thought her to be older at first because of the baby, but I think she's still a young lass. If it's any consolation to you, Eddie was complaining he got nothing from her. I think you get the meaning."

"Glad to hear it. I think she's young too. Well, it's been a long day."

"I concur with that. Good night."

"Good night, Captain."

Harrison climbed into the wagon. He wanted to get under the quilt before she fell asleep and there wasn't room left for him.

CHAPTER FIVE

*I*t was strange to share the tick mattress with Harrison. At first she tried to keep any part of her from touching him but the inside of the wagon was extremely small. Her muscles began to cramp and she had to relax. The next thing she knew she was on her side leaning against Harrison.

He put his arm loosely around her waist and she waited. He did nothing more. She relaxed more and found Harrison to be very comfortable. He had all his clothes on, and her relief was so great a few tears fell.

"It's going to be fine," he whispered into the dark night.

"I know. Thank you for taking my side and helping me. I haven't had that happen very often."

"Get some sleep." He moved around a bit, probably trying to get comfortable, and the next thing she heard was light snoring.

She wanted to laugh. It never occurred to her he might snore. Thankfully, it wasn't as loud as she'd heard in the saloon. Her thoughts drifted toward his reaction when she had mentioned being married before. How long had he been

married? Had his wife died? When? He didn't have kids…
unless he had left them with a relative. It confused her that a
man was sleeping next to her and she didn't know much
about him. He made her feel safe, though, and he hadn't said
that today had been her fault. He did say *"our daughter"* when
referring to Essie. Her heart glowed. Essie hadn't even been
born in the saloon. That should count for something. Right?

At the sound of soft footfalls on snow outside the wagon,
Cora tensed.

"Harrison," a man whispered, loud enough to wake him.
"Your turn for guard duty."

Harrison sat up, eased away from her, and grabbed his
rifle. He opened the back and climbed out. He took the time
to close the canvas back up. There hadn't been a grumble or
groan out of him. He certainly differed from the men she'd
seen before.

She fell back to sleep until Essie woke her. Cora fed the
baby and burped her and then sat and studied her. Her little
one sure was growing fast. She must ask about the linseed to
waterproof the outside of the diaper. It sounded fascinating.
She had so much to learn.

She finished with Essie and climbed out of the wagon,
grabbed her clothes off the line, and then climbed back in.
Clean clothes had become a luxury. Once outside again she
started the fire and put gingerbread into the Dutch oven to
cook. It could be tricky, but she'd watched the cook at the
saloon prepare food each morning. Next, she sliced some
bacon and fried it up. She needed enough for breakfast plus
the noon meal.

She saw coffee beans and smiled. The smile widened
when she saw the coffee mill. Harrison had made some of the
best coffee she ever had and now she knew why. She roasted
the beans, ground them, added a pinch of salt to keep it from
getting bitter and poured water from the water barrel that

hung on the side of the wagon. She'd fill the barrel after breakfast.

She took down and folded the clothes as things cooked. Then she dropped the rope and collected the poles and put them in the wagon.

Eddie walked by and then stopped and sauntered toward her. "I'd consider it payment for using me if you cooked my meals for me. It's the least you can do. You wouldn't even have Essie if not for me." He glowered at her.

Her jaw dropped. Wasn't she done with him? "You must talk to Harrison. It's his food." She walked to the tailgate, ready to put out the tin plates.

A heavy hand fell on her shoulder and she jumped as Eddie gave her a punishing squeeze. "Feed me *now*."

"Let go of me," she hissed.

"Get away from my wife, Connor," Harrison growled.

"She was mine before she was yours. I saw you go into the wagon to lie with her last night. She's a wildcat if you know what I mean."

Harrison's eyes narrowed. "Get away from me and my family before I do something I'll regret."

"You didn't regret last night, did you?"

Captain London rode up. "Eddie, you have no stake in this wagon. Go back to your own. I want you to leave Mrs. Walsh alone."

Eddie threw dark look at her before he left.

"What was that about?" the captain asked.

"He thinks I should cook his meals for him as payment for traveling in his wagon." Cora looked down at her hands.

The captain laughed. "See you later." He rode off.

Harrison took her hands in his. "Did he hurt you?"

Her shoulder throbbed. "I'm fine. He didn't pack enough food. He thought the amount of food the captain told him to haul was exaggerated. He'll have enough for a few more weeks if he's not greedy. He should have listened. He doesn't have tools to fix his wagon either."

"Maybe people will help him along the way," Harrison mused. Then he smiled and gave an appreciative sniff. "Breakfast looks good."

Cora took the Dutch oven she had piled hot coals on and cleaned it off. She put it on the tailgate and opened the lid. The gingerbread was perfect, and she felt proud of herself. She sliced a big piece for Harrison and put plenty of bacon on his plate.

"I was hoping to get some milk from one of the others but... Gingerbread is much better with butter."

"It's good just the way it is. I can't remember the last time I had gingerbread." He smiled and took another bite. "I have a question for you. How old are you?"

"A few of the married women are sixteen. It's not unusual for a woman to marry young."

"No it's not," he said, angling his head and giving her an assessing look. "But you didn't answer my question."

"I'm eighteen as of two weeks ago. I left the saloon before Madam Grealy had a chance to gather men to pay for me. The orphanage told her I was ten when they sold me to her. I was almost twelve and small for my age. One of the girls who worked there told me to let her think I was ten. I did not understand at the time why."

"She thought you to be fifteen when you and Eddie got together?"

"Yes." She stood and gathered all the dirty dishes and pans. "I'll go down to the creek and wash these."

"Use the water from the barrel. I'll fill it."

"I'll be careful—"

"I don't want you around the other women for a while. Most of them act as though they drink vinegar all day."

She laughed. "I've never heard that one before. It's true."

Harrison poured water into two clean pans and left with the barrel. It didn't take her long to get everyone ready to travel. She adjusted her big poke bonnet and her sling and then she carefully lifted Essie and placed her in the sling.

"All set?" Harrison attached the water to the outside of the wagon. "Let me help you up."

"Would it make you mad if I walked for a bit? I've spent too much time jostling in that wagon, and my bones ache."

He smiled. "Stay where I can see you and signal if you need to feed Essie or if you grow tired."

She felt as though he had given her a gift. "Thank you." She began her walk. The wagons would pass her by soon enough. Her bones ached, but her shoulder pained something awful. She wouldn't be able to switch the sling to the injured shoulder.

WHEW, she was eighteen. Cora was right, many married at sixteen, but he'd been around sixteen-year-olds and he wanted someone more mature. She didn't seem the type who would think there'd be a big house waiting for her in Oregon. He'd heard a few women talk about what furniture they'd order, what curtains they would hang, even about rugs in their sitting rooms.

He'd be making the furniture for his family. Family: he hadn't planned on one and never wanted one since Ora died. He had to admit Cora and her problems had kept him busy, and it saddened him some to realize he didn't think of Ora as much. But though his pain had lessened, it was still there.

One of these times he'd get up the nerve to ask about Essie's father. Part of him didn't want the truth but the other part needed it. If they were to trust each other, they needed to be truthful. That didn't mean he'd have to ask right away.

Cora had been through enough in her life, and if someone had attacked her…

There wasn't a thing he could do about it now. It didn't matter. Besides, if she had been attacked, he'd feel bad for her and he needed Ora in his heart not Cora. He hadn't noticed before, but their names were almost the same. Strange.

Three hours later, he caught her signal to him and pulled off the line. She caught up a bit out of breath but she looked rosier than ever.

"I need to feed Essie."

"I thought maybe you were tired," he teased.

"A little, I confess. I usually alternate shoulders with the sling but—" She put her hand over her mouth as she stared at him.

"I'll lift you both into the back, and I want to see your shoulder after you feed Essie."

Cora didn't look happy, but she nodded. He got back up on the bench and joined the end of the line. They'd be eating dust from the other wagons the rest of the day.

He waited a reasonable amount of time and glanced over his shoulder. Essie was in her basket. He looked forward again.

"Give me your hand so I can climb over and sit with you," she said.

He helped her and waited. Then she unbuttoned the front of her dress and pulled the brown fabric down away from her shoulder. She glanced away.

Her shoulder was a fiery red color where it wasn't turning black and blue. He gently touched it and she flinched.

"What happened?" He tried to control the anger in his voice.

"Eddie. He grabbed my shoulder when he told me I was to feed him and he didn't let go until you came back."

"Why didn't you say something? That looks painful."

"I didn't want to start a fight between the two of you and then the captain was there. It hurts but I've had worse. It'll heal."

"Worse?"

"They smacked me in the face, punched me in the stomach, and one time they broke my arm at the saloon. They didn't like it when I tried to sneak out or talked back to them. I got through it. Like I said, I'll heal."

He leaned over and placed a kiss on her shoulder. "If anyone touches you again I want to know about it. I'm your husband, and I will protect both you and our daughter."

"You said it again." She sounded pleased.

"Said what?"

"*Our daughter.* I thought it was, well I wasn't sure if you realized you said it. I didn't want to hope too much and then be crushed."

"Look at me, Cora. I am Essie's father and you are my wife."

Tears welled in her eyes.

"Awe, don't cry."

"I'm sorry. I can't help it." She sniffed.

Not having a clue what to say, he just continued to drive the oxen.

Finally they were circling for the night. Essie woke just in time. He put on the brake and tied off the lines. Once he helped Cora to turn and get into the back, he walked to the front of the wagon. He needed to unyoke the oxen, make sure their feet were fine and they were watered and fed. Then off to his horses and cattle.

He'd hired two brothers and their friend to tend the livestock, and they were doing an excellent job. One drove his second wagon while the other two drove the animals. They rotated jobs and took their turns at guard duty. He'd been lucky. They'd all heard about men who were hired to take care of animals stealing them away in the night.

He asked Zander, Heath, and Declan to come by the fire for supper the next night to meet his wife and daughter. The three men accepted cheerfully.

Good, now that was done, he needed to tend his wife's shoulder. He'd like nothing more than to punch Eddie Connor, but such behavior wouldn't leave Cora in a good light. There were always too many people watching in the party.

Out of the corner of his eye, he saw Cora bending and picking up firewood. He hustled her way. "I've got that. You go rest."

She frowned, almost as though she was disappointed.

"Are you going into the woods? I'd like to go if possible. There's something calming about walking among the trees."

He took the dried branches from her. "Come on." They walked, and he picked up more firewood as they went. "I invited Zander, Heath and Declan to join us for supper tomorrow. Would that be fine with you?"

"I don't think I've met them."

"Probably not. They tend my livestock and drive the extra wagon."

"Extra wagon? Why would you need two wagons?"

"Spare parts for the wagons, extra tools for when we get there. Also food for the boys."

"Boys? Just how old are you, Harrison?"

"Older than you, for sure."

"How much older?" She stared at him with teasing eyes.

"I'm twenty-seven, if you must know."

"Oh, I didn't know you were so old. You look like you're still in your prime."

He laughed loudly, and a flock of birds took flight. Then they both laughed and when they stopped, they stared into each other's eyes. His urge to kiss her lips was so strong, and he took a step forward. Luckily Essie cried, or he would have gotten in over his head.

Cora lifted the baby out of her sling and kissed her cheek before she held her against her shoulder. She cooed to Essie and after an initial squirming, Essie settled back to sleep.

"You're good with her."

He found her blush endearing. He needed to get out of these woods. Things were happening too fast, and the secluded hush of the nature surrounding them was not helping to keep his wits about him.

WHY WAS Harrison looking at her in such a strange way? Almost as if he found her… pleasing? He was a good man, she reminded herself, and she was lucky to have him. She had fallen in love with him the first time he said *"our daughter."* She just hadn't realized it. What were his dreams for Oregon? Or was he going to California? They had spent more time together, yet she didn't know very much. They still had months, she supposed, but she wanted to know sooner. He had men working for him, and she hadn't known it.

In all fairness, though, she hadn't told him about Rudy. And knowing about his wife would be a good thing, wouldn't it? He must still love her—as well he should, but… She was grateful for what she had. She sent up a quick prayer of thanks and praise to the Lord.

She set out everything she needed to make potato cakes and bacon, and she found preserves in the wagon she planned to top the cornbread with. She filled a pot with beans and poured water over them for the next evening. Some men planned to go hunting the next day, and she looked forward to whatever they might bring back. Something other than bacon would be a wonderful change.

She had everything just about ready when Harrison came back to camp. He smiled and kissed her cheek. "I want to check your shoulder after we eat."

She nodded and served him a plateful of food. He sat on a crate and took a bite of everything.

"You are really a good cook. Better than—" His brow wrinkled and his eyes grew sad. "You're a good cook." He was a bit subdued while they ate.

He was thinking about his wife. He must be. Cora felt for him. Would she always stand in his wife's shadow? Would everything she did be compared to her?

"What was her name?"

"Ora. She was as pretty as she was kind. We grew up together, and it was just natural for us to marry. We had such hope for this trip. The farm we'd shared with my parents and three brothers had gotten crowded and everyone thought they knew best. I wanted to raise horses and cattle so we saved and saved, and we were excited to go to Oregon and make a fresh start. Ora kept hoping for a child, and my mother didn't help any, announcing that Ora still wasn't pregnant every month. We'd bought the wagons, and Ora was washing clothes for all of us. She was watching me, not paying attention to the fire. Her skirt caught fire, and she started running—away from me." He stopped as though lost in thought. "She was in so much pain; it was a blessing when she died."

"I'm so sorry, Harrison. I shouldn't have asked. It's not my business."

He shook his head. "It is your business. It's just hard to talk about. I used to feel her around me all the time but lately I haven't been thinking about her as much as I did, and that makes me feel like I'm not honoring her memory. She hasn't even been dead three months, and already I'm…" He wiped his hand over his face. "I'm going to check on the livestock."

Cora gathered the dirty dishes. All she'd brought Harrison was pain and more responsibility. She knew all she wanted to know and wished she hadn't asked. Maybe she needed to keep her distance, but she wasn't the one who reached for his hand or kissed his cheek.

She finished washing everything when she remembered Harrison said they'd have to act happily married. She'd read too much into the little things he did. He wanted to be alone. She climbed into the wagon, put on her nightgown, fed Essie, and lay down. She left the lantern lit and put it near the end of the wagon so he could get what he needed. Her heart hurt for her and for Harrison. Ora was a permanent part of their marriage. He needed to be left alone, and she could do that.

She listened to the sounds of the camp. Men debating how long it would take for them to get to Fort Laramie. Women trying to round up their children for bed. She heard a woman crying, and her husband trying to comfort her. Farther away she could hear laughter and the noise one husband made as he berated his wife.

A sigh slipped past her lips. Just because Harrison had married her didn't mean he even liked her much. He liked Essie, though. It was better than being with Eddie. It was understandable that Harrison was in mourning. She should have known and not badgered him. He was cheated by the death of his love, and now he'd live his and Ora's dream with Cora instead.

Would people in Oregon treat her as an outcast? Word was bound to get out she had once lived in a saloon. What would life be for Essie?

"Cora?"

"Did you need something, Harrison?" She hoped he just wanted to say good night.

"I need to tend your shoulder."

"Harrison you don't have to do anything. I respect that you're mourning, and I'll try to stay out of your way."

The wagon rocked as he climbed in. He reached into a crate and grabbed the jar of salve. He kneeled in the tight space and helped her to sit up. Then he bared her shoulder and hissed. "I swear it looks worse."

"The bruising is just darkening, is all." She tried her best not to glance at him, but it was a battle easily lost. His lips formed a grim line. "I can do it," she insisted.

"Woman, would you please let me take care of you?" His voice sounded beseeching as his gaze bored into hers.

A chill rolled over her body, and her breath hitched as she nodded. His touch was gentle as he put the salve on her shoulder, but it raised goose bumps. "It's getting cold out, I think."

He smiled as though she said something funny. "I'm finished." He raised her gown to cover her shoulder and kissed her forehead. "Thank you for leaving the lantern lit for me. I don't think anyone has done that for me before."

Before she knew it, he was out of the wagon. A smile played on her lips. He was so hard to understand, but one day she'd figure him out. Her eyes were almost closed when she realized she hadn't made the dough for the bread. She always made it at night, and by morning the dough had raised and was ready to bake.

She secured her shawl around her and climbed out of the wagon and then put the tailgate down. The light from the dying fire was barely enough for her to see, but she'd made the bread many times. She mixed all the ingredients and was kneading the dough when she saw a shadow. She had a feeling Harrison wouldn't be happy.

"Cora? What, pray tell, are you doing? Morning is hours away."

"I need to have the dough ready to bake for tomorrow. We're having guests for supper," she whispered.

"Oh. In that case move over. I can knead it quicker, and I bet it's hurting your shoulder."

She opened her eyes wide and scooted over. He knew what he was doing and he was done in a matter of minutes. He handed the dough to her, and she put it in a bowl and covered it with a dish cloth.

"Thank you," she whispered.

He cradled her face in his hands and gazed into her eyes. After a moment, his lips twitched. "You are full of surprises, but you do me proud." He kissed her forehead again before he turned away.

She stared after him, wondering what had gotten into him. She quickly cleaned up and climbed back into the wagon. *"You do me proud."* Just what he meant by that was a mystery, but she held onto the words that made her so happy.

CHAPTER SIX

*I*t never occurred to him that Zander, Heath and Declan would find his wife attractive enough to watch her every move. Harrison smiled. Cora didn't seem to notice them. She kept glancing at him for approval.

"Where are you all from?" she asked as she sliced up the roasted elk meat and poured gravy on it.

"We come from Ireland," Zander answered. "We've been in America for over a year now. I met these two down at the docks. Heath and Declan have been my best mates."

"How nice." She sliced the bread and when she presented the butter she looked especially happy. "It's the first butter I've made on the trip. Harrison brought me some milk this morning, and all I had to do was pour it into the butter churn. The constant movement of the wagon turned it into butter. Can you imagine?"

"It's the first we've seen too, ma'am," Heath said.

She served them elk with gravy, beans and bread with butter. When she sat down, she glanced at Harrison again. He smiled, and she blushed.

Harrison said grace. They began to eat, and it was the best

meal she'd made so far. The elk was tender, and the gravy went down too soon. He wished he had the patience to savor it but they all ate fairly quickly.

She got up while they still ate and pulled the Dutch oven out of the coals. "I made an apple crisp with some dried apples. I hope you saved room."

Harrison wanted to laugh at the looks on the boys' faces. He might have thought it was Christmas by the way their eyes glowed.

After she served them each two helpings of the crisp, she made sure they all had coffee before she sat next to Harrison. This time it seemed she sat closer to him. Maybe she noticed how they watched her.

Declan was first to stand. "Ma'am, would you like help with the dishes?"

"I think my wife and I can handle it. You're our guests."

"Thank you for the fine food, Mrs. Walsh," Zander said as he stood and put his plate on the tailgate. "We have work to do, but it's been a pleasure."

Heath and Declan put their empty plates and cups on the tailgate and said their thanks before they left.

"You look amused," she said.

"They were practically falling over their feet to impress you."

"I doubt that, but I think the food turned out well."

He smiled and shook his head. "It was the best meal I've had since we've been out here."

"The elk made the difference." She gathered the plates and set them with the others. Before she reached for the pans she used to wash dishes, he stood right behind her and turned her around.

"*You* made the difference. You were the perfect hostess, and the meal was outstanding. Like I said last night you do me proud." He wrapped his arms around her and drew her close. "How's your shoulder?"

She put her cheek against him. "It'll get better."

They stood there for a few minutes before he drew back and kissed her cheek. "I have first watch. I will put on another pot of coffee to boil."

"I can do it."

"I know you can. So can I." He took the coffee mill out of her hand and laughed. "Really, I can do this, you can wash the dishes."

He ground up the beans, put the water over it and put it on to boil. Then he watched as Cora took a pinch of salt and added it to the pot.

"You are kindhearted, Mrs. Walsh." He walked away before she looked up. He kept walking until he was alone, not a soul in sight.

Ora, either I make this a good marriage or lose it all. She's not what I thought when I married her. I never intended to even like her. She's growing on me, Ora, and it's not fair to you. I miss you, darlin'. I just wish I knew what to do. I thought I could ignore her, but she enchants me and little Essie needs a father. I feel so good one minute, and then I'm in misery thinking of you knowing what I'm doing. I love you, Ora.

He stared out at the vast land and sighed. It seemed like a promise of what would be waiting in Oregon. He'd go back and grab the coffee pot and a cup and start guard duty early. He didn't trust himself not to kiss Cora's lips.

"Harrison, get up. Zander is hurt."

Cora wasn't sure who was out there, but his voice sounded urgent. How hurt was Zander? She stripped off her blanket and crawled to the back of the wagon. But Harrison and the other man were already gone.

She wouldn't get any more sleep tonight. Each night she set out her clothes to put on in the morning. She groped for those she had lain out earlier. After quickly dressing, she checked on Essie. She was sleeping in longer intervals each night. As silent as she could, Cora climbed down and got the fire going. Next, she put down the tailgate and grabbed a satchel Harrison had shown her. It was full of things for illness and accidents.

She wanted to heat water in case they would need willow bark tea or water to wash him. Maybe they wouldn't even bring Zander to this wagon. They might have gone to Mrs. Chapman's.

She filled her biggest pot with water and set it on a metal grate that sat in the fire. Then she found the coffee pot and quickly roasted some beans before grinding them in the mill. After dumping the grounds into the pot, she poured the water and put the coffee on the grate next to the other pot.

The dough she'd started earlier was ready, and she set it in the Dutch oven. As soon as the fire went down a bit, she'd bake the bread. Zander was the one with dark brown hair and blue eyes, she recalled. He'd seemed nice enough. What was it like to leave the country he was born in and travel to America?

She peered into the darkness. There was still no sign of the men. She took the crates out to use for chairs and retrieved Essie from the wagon, basket and all. Essie looked a lot like Rudy, and a pang went through her thinking about him. He'd been such a sweet man, well boy teetering on the edge of becoming a man. Life could be cruel, very cruel indeed. Loving her had gotten him killed. The knowledge of it haunted her.

"Mrs. Walsh!" Heath ran toward her. "Harrison said to

ready the wagon for Zander. He'll need to lie down and he said to put his oilcloth over the straw ticking to keep the blood from seeping into the mattress." Heath was out of breath when he finished.

"Sit next to the baby and I'll get the wagon prepared." She snatched up Harrison's bedroll and laid it out. She grabbed the oilcloth and climbed into the wagon. She covered the ticking and made sure there were blankets and cloths nearby. She jumped back out and cleaned off the tailgate. Then she filled a cup with water and handed it to Heath.

"What happened?"

"He was sleeping by the cattle and somehow they all started to stampede right at him. I've seen nothing like it. The cattle didn't even go far. Just far enough to stomp poor Zander."

"Oh my, I see them now. Why did they put a piece of wood in his mouth?"

"To help keep him from screaming."

She felt the blood drain from her face. The smell of blood permeated the air, turning her stomach some, but she stood strong.

"Heath, pull out some trunks so we have enough room to tend to him," Harrison called out.

Heath pulled the trunks and crates out quickly and then got back into the wagon to hold Zander under his head and shoulders to place him on the straw tick. Declan looked worried. Harrison's expression was one of stone.

Someone must have roused Mrs. Chapman, who hurried to the wagon. "You'll all need to get out so I can tend to him. Cora I'll need hot water. And does anyone have morphine? This is going to hurt something awful, and I'll need him still. It looks like one leg, an arm, and ribs are broken. Harrison, I will need your strength to wrap the bandages and to reset his leg."

Cora grabbed the basin and poured some of the hot water into it and handed it to Mrs. Chapman along with clean cloths. Cora exchanged glances with Harrison. He gave her the slightest of nods which gave her the courage to climb into the wagon and start washing away as much blood as she could.

Heath and Declan rinsed blood out of the cloths, as much as would come out. Cora glanced up and Harrison had Essie in one arm while he poured coffee for everyone.

He handed two of the cups to her. "Captain London has morphine. He'll be here in a minute."

Mrs. Chapman's shoulders relaxed. "Thank you, Harrison," she said. Then she whispered to Cora, "You have a good man there."

"I know."

"What in tarnation happened?" Captain London thundered when he reached the wagon. He handed the morphine to Cora.

Mrs. Chapman took the wooden stick out of Zander's mouth and poured a bit of morphine into his mouth. He swallowed it quickly followed by a cup of water Harrison had handed to Cora.

"Cora, switch places with Harrison. I'll need you other two boys to help hold him down." Mrs. Chapman took out all the instruments in her bag and threaded a needle.

Cora crawled to the back of the wagon. Harrison was there to lift her down. He held her to him for a moment before he climbed in. She hurried over to the fire and checked on Essie. She was sleeping through it. Captain London was back with a full pot of coffee.

"I figured we'd need this." He put it at the edge of the fire on the grate along with the pot Cora made. "People are getting up and around. I'll let them know we're leaving a bit later."

"We're not going to stay here a day or two? Zander looks terrible."

"It's simply not possible to keep stopping every time someone is hurt. It's early in the trip but as we go along, you'll see what I mean. There will be sickness, accidents, and women will have babies. The main thing is to get over the mountains before the snow falls and makes crossing impossible."

Cora nodded as though she understood, but she didn't. There was nothing easy about riding in the back of the wagon, being jostled and sometimes the holes were so bad she was separated from the bottom of the wagon and set back down with a bruising thump.

She heard Zander scream, and then his screams weren't as loud. He must be biting on the wood again. She didn't know much about cattle, but they were large and certainly extremely heavy.

"I need you boys to hold him still while I set his arm."

Cora shuddered. She took her bread out of the coals and peeked at it. It looked perfect. At least they'd have something to eat when they were done.

The woman from the next wagon walked over with a plate of bacon and pancakes. "Howdy. I'm Sally Waverly. I thought some food would come in handy." She put the big plate on one crate and then peeked at Essie. "Oh my, she's as cute as can be." She smiled at Cora. "My Rod will be over soon to hitch up your oxen, Mrs. Walsh."

"It's so kind of you. Please, call me Cora, and this here is Essie. I know Harrison will appreciate the help. Zander was run over by some cows. He's in bad shape."

"He'll be riding in the wagon, I bet."

"He most certainly will. Poor man," Cora agreed. "It'll be days of bouncing in that wooden contraption."

"Some call it a rolling home, but I think I like wooden

contraption better," Sally said. "If you need anything, don't hesitate to ask. I know you're a new mother and wife and it sounded as though your upbringing might not have been one that taught you many domestic chores."

Fiery heat bloomed across Cora's face.

"I didn't mean to offend you," Sally hastened to add. "Everyone seems to have a story they are leaving behind. Me, I grew up on a farm. I was an orphan and the old farmer and his wife took me and used me as a field hand. They never adopted me. It's been a long road, and I've had so many people help me through, I thought I'd be able to show you a few of the things they taught me."

Cora searched Sally's face for any sign of teasing but the green-eyed blond looked sincere. "Thank you, Sally. There is a lot I don't know."

"Between you and me, there are many that don't have enough skills. Some seek help but others are too prideful I guess. Husbands have told me that their wives are capable. Your first husband…" She shook her head. "That didn't come out right. Eddie was one who asked me not to speak to you."

A burly man ambled up to the fire and smiled at Sally.

"Oh, Cora, this is my husband Rod."

"Nice to meet you, ma'am." He tipped his hat to her, and she smiled at the dark-haired, dark-eyed man. Both the Waverlys looked to be not much older than Cora. He walked over to the wagon and conferred with Harrison for a moment and then left, likely in search of the oxen.

Willow bark tea was made, and the belongings they had taken out of the wagon were placed in the second wagon. No one wanted to move Zander. Harrison had the morphine up front with him for when it was needed.

Harrison thought it best he take the end of the line. He'd told her he wanted to go slow for Zander but also so he could stop and get her onto the bench when Essie was hungry.

Cora smiled as she walked alongside the slow-moving wagon. Harrison's words of caring, filled her with happiness.

Her happiness continued until they stopped for the night. Then concern abruptly struck. Where was she supposed to sleep? There wasn't enough room in the back of the wagon for her and Essie. It probably wasn't proper anyway. She would have to make sure to ask Harrison. Checking their supplies, she decided salt pork and beans would work for supper. At least she hoped the beans were still soaking.

There was still enough bread, but she needed to make more than one loaf if she was to feed Zander, Declan, and Heath. Getting everything ready with Zander staring at her through pain-filled eyes was disturbing, but she managed. It wasn't until she was kneading the dough for the next day that she realized he probably didn't even know he was looking at her. Morphine was strong medicine. They'd been able to give him less because of the willow bark tea.

After everyone ate, *the boys* as Harrison called them, talked to Zander, keeping him company. Cora put Essie in her sling and washed the dishes. There was the tent, she realized. She could sleep there while Harrison would more than likely want to sleep under the wagon in case Zander needed something during the night.

And she was right. Harrison put up the tent and arranged the things she'd need inside. She relaxed. It would be just fine. Then she saw him put an extra blanket inside. He smiled at her, and she smiled back. He was thoughtful; it probably was colder in the tent than in the wagon.

"I'd better get some shut-eye. I have guard duty tonight," Heath said.

Why was Heath carrying his bedroll to the wagon? He

rolled it out and then rolled himself on top of it, under the wagon.

Declan stood up. "I have first shift. I offered to do two shifts. Both Heath and I offered to take longer shifts because Zander is laid up. Some men haven't even taken their turns yet. Imagine that. I know as drovers we're expected to take guard duty. We do every night, especially since Harrison has the most cattle, but we've been on our trip long enough for all to have taken a turn. Not the cattle, mind you, but the people." He shook his head and headed into the dark.

"He didn't mean that the cattle pull guard duty," Harrison said seriously.

"I… well, I didn't think—I knew what he meant."

Apparently, Harrison didn't think she was very smart.

He chuckled. "I was teasing you."

Tilting her head she studied her handsome husband. "I thought teasing to be mean spirited."

"Not all." He banked the fire and offered her his hand.

"I'm not tired," she told him. "You go on." How was she supposed to sleep in the tent with him? The one time in the wagon had confused her. She didn't want confusion to cloud her mind.

"Humor me. I can't leave you out here alone."

Essie took that moment to make a small cry. "I do need to feed her." Cora took his hand and stood. Then she followed him, and when he lifted the canvas open she went into the tent. She took Essie out of the sling and set her on the quilt, and then she sat next to her and unbuttoned her dress. She used her shawl to cover herself and Essie while nursing. Harrison would have turned his head away. He was a gentleman. She didn't need to worry. He waited outside of the tent until Essie was done and Cora was in her night clothes with the quilt pulled up to her chin.

He came in and just like in the wagon, he made the tent seem so much smaller.

"You're sleeping here?" Her voice sounded like a squeak to her.

He didn't answer. Instead he unbuttoned his shirt, and Cora immediately closed her eyes tight. He slipped under the covers and a shiver went through her.

"You're wearing a nightgown," he commented.

"Of course I am."

"I'm wearing my union suit, so you can open your eyes." Amusement danced in his voice.

"I don't know why, but it scares me and I'm sorry. We are married and—"

He kissed her on the lips. His very masculine lips were gentle. She liked it and it muddled her thoughts to no end. Rudy's kiss had been so hard and insistent that it sometimes hurt. Harrison moved his lips a bit and she lifted her head, not wanting the kiss to end. She put her arms around his neck to keep him close. She let out a sigh of pleasure and then instantly let go and moved off.

What was she doing? She was just a stand in for his beloved Ora. She turned on her side and faced away from him. To her surprise, he closed the distance between them and put his arm over her waist, drawing her back against him as he whispered, "Good night, sweet."

As if she would get any sleep after that.

CHAPTER SEVEN

*T*he tall grass of the prairie was at first something intriguing, something different to look at. But it sure made for some tough going. Harrison was constantly peering behind him, trying to locate Cora and Essie. It made for some difficulty walking too. They traveled with the Platte River to their right. It seemed very inviting as the days began to get warmer. It was almost time for the nooning, and stopping, however briefly, would be a Godsend. Zander groaned several times as they went over ruts and rocks.

They rarely circled for the noon meal. They just unhitched the animals and brought them to where they could find grass to eat and water to drink.

He watched Cora shyly smile at him as she approached the wagon. She'd been shy for the last week, ever since he kissed her. Her blushing face intrigued him. Certainly she'd been kissed before. She did have Essie.

"Do you think we'll stop by the river for a few days?" Cora asked as she repositioned Essie.

"I doubt it. The water is muddy. If you use it you have to haul it and wait for the sand and silt to fall to the bottom."

"In case of an emergency, I suppose."

Harrison took off his hat and wiped his forehead with his sleeve. "Water supply has a lot of factors for each wagon. Such as, did they fill the water barrel when there was good water? How many people are in their family? Is there water for the animals? There will be times when we must share water with the oxen. We have plenty for this part of the trip but if you want to wash anything you'll have to use the Platte water."

She handed him sliced biscuits with bacon in between the slices and then fixed a plate for Zander. "Here, take Essie while I climb in."

Harrison always enjoyed holding Essie. He loved to just stare at her little features and touch her little fingers and toes. She'd taken up a big part of his heart. He picked up the dipper and lowered it into the water barrel on the side of the wagon. He filled two cups, one that he handed to Cora for Zander and one for him.

He learned to wait until Cora was done before getting her water. It stayed cooler in the barrel. He sat and ate while talking to Essie. Usually he asked her about her mother. Why she liked things this way and didn't like certain other things. Essie never took sides. She just waved her hands and stared at him.

Women had begun to put linseed oil on the diapers. A few asked Cora's advice. It made her happy, though why they didn't know about waterproofing diapers he had no idea. Mrs. Swatt shared her pattern for flannel diaper covers for when the baby slept. No more smelly ticks or blankets. She'd also shown Cora how to make biscuits. But their visits had dropped off.

"How's Zander? He slept more of the morning."

"He's healing. I haven't seen any signs of infection, but Mrs. Chapman will be the final judge on that this evening."

They saw Heath, Declan, and Captain London heading their way. "I'd best get busy making more biscuits with bacon."

"How's the patient?" Captain London asked as he drew near.

"Resting and healing," Harrison told him.

Cora handed them each a plate of food and offered cold coffee or water. Harrison gave thanks and they started eating.

"Everyone is saying we're in Indian country," Heath blurted out.

"I heard it too," Declan said. He nodded his head as his eyes grew wide.

"Now hold on. There have been no problems reported. Fort Laramie isn't all that far away." Captain London put his plate down on a nearby crate. "I don't want to hear that rumors are spreading." He picked up his plate, took a seat on the crate, and took a hearty bite.

"Yes, sir," both Declan and Heath each replied as they sat and dug into their own plates.

After he finished eating, the captain wiped his mouth with his sleeve. "You'll want to start collecting buffalo chips on this part of the trip." He stood and put his plate and cup on the tailgate. "Thank you, Mrs. Walsh. It was a treat as always."

Harrison had noticed almost from the start of the trip that Captain London never did his own cooking. As long as he complimented the women, he never needed to cook for himself. It was a smart way to go about it. He had two scouts, but he never ate with them.

The nooning was almost over, and Harrison hadn't had but a second alone with his family. He wanted to ask Cora a few questions. His feelings for her were getting stronger, and he was afraid of being called a fool.

Before he knew it he had to hitch up the team. Cora

smiled at him as she walked. The long grass gave way to sand unlike anything he'd ever seen, and the women walking struggled to walk.

One scout rode down the line letting each driver know that they were going a bit longer than usual today. The scout rode away before Harrison had a chance to ask why. But soon enough the reason became clear.

He drove by grave after grave, most looking fresh. It was a depressing sight.

———

CORA WATCHED as the scout stopped by each wagon. When he got to the last one, he turned to go back to the head of the line. She heard him slow as he neared her and wanted to groan. He stared at her in a lewd fashion and spoke to her too often. If only Harrison would warn the other man off, but he didn't. Unlike Eddie, Harrison didn't care who she talked to.

"You do know that I could give you a ride. I'd put you in front of me with my arms around you. You'd be safe."

"Safe from what? Besides, I have a husband."

"Heard tell you changed husbands on this trip. Maybe I could be next?"

She ignored him and tried to walk forward but he zigged zagged his mount in front of her slowing her down.

"*Your husband* will have guard duty one of these nights. You'll be in that tent all alone."

Everything about him made her stomach churn. "Leave me alone."

"I can be very quiet—"

"Leave me alone!" she shrieked.

Harrison pulled out of line.

"Mr. Walsh has pulled off and is waiting for me."

This time he let her go around him. She hurried to the wagon, dismayed to find herself shaking by the time she got there.

Harrison went to her side of the wagon to lift her up. "What happened? You're trembling."

"Let's get back in line."

He nodded and lifted both she and the baby up. Then he rounded the wagon and climbed onto the bench seat. He unwrapped the lines from around the brake and yelled, "Haw!"

The wagon lurched forward, and they rode without speaking for several moments. The tremors began to calm, and only an occasional tremor rippled through her.

"Did you want to tell me what that was all about?" Harrison broke the silence. "You were very loud."

She stared at him as her heart dropped. He thought she'd done something. "Tom Simps was propositioning me. Nothing new except I was madder than usual and he wouldn't let me pass him."

Harrison's fingers tightened on the reins, but he stared at the wagon in front of him. He didn't even glance at her. Didn't offer even a hint of outrage at the other man's behavior or a murmur of understanding for her predicament of being caught with him.

"We're going extra-long today," Harrison said in a terse tone.

Turning her head she ignored him.

"You probably saw all the graves. There must be sickness in the area. I noticed most of the women are staying very close to their wagons."

"Oh," she said without turning back.

"Didn't it seem strange you were walking alone?" he asked with a faint edge of irritation. "Or have people been avoiding you again?"

The pain couldn't have been worse if he'd struck her. Had she done something wrong? Were people gossiping about her again? The group she walked with a week ago had dwindled down to almost no one. She hadn't noticed they were staying close to their wagons.

She watched the river as they went by. No matter where she went or what she did, she'd be judged harshly. Though she had to admit, Harrison judging her that way was a hurtful surprise.

She kept thinking and thinking about what she might have done to deserve his scorn.

She had gone to pick flowers yesterday, and Tom Simps said he'd been sent to find her. Was that it? People had seen her coming out of the tall grass with Simps? There had to be more. People had been avoiding her all week. Had Mrs. Chapman given her a curious look last night?

She snuck a peek at Harrison, and he stared ahead, his face set like stone. Her stomach churned. Quickly, she took Essie from the sling and handed her to Harrison. Then she jumped off the side and was sick. She had eaten little for the noon meal, but that didn't stop her stomach from continuing to heave.

A few who went by congratulated her, but she did not understand why. She stood there with her head bent until she heard a horse race toward her. It was Simps again. This time he didn't ask, he lifted her up and put her right in front of him. Fighting him would only cause a scene.

Tears filled her eyes as they approached her wagon.

"Missing something, Harrison?" Simps asked.

"Is she hurt?" Harrison wasn't looking at her at all. He slowed the wagon, so it was barely moving, and Simps set her on the bench.

She'd held her breath, afraid she'd fall. How dare they think that putting her in the wagon while it was moving was a good idea? Harrison had always made her feel like a woman with value but now…

They passed more graves, and her tears wouldn't wait a minute more. She reset Essie in her sling and turned away.

Harrison cleared his throat. "I suspect there is a sickness going around, and Captain London wants us away from it." His voice was tense, and a shiver rippled along Cora's spine.

She didn't answer or look at him for the rest of the day. She'd thought of him as her hero, but right now he was so cold toward her there was nothing heroic about him. If she had a home, she'd go to it, curl up with Essie, and have a good cry.

It was getting darker and darker, but they still went on. She wouldn't be able to make food in the dark. There wasn't anything left from the day to eat, and what about the morning? She'd have to ask Sally. Cora's shoulders slumped lower. Harrison had made it clear no one wanted to have anything to do with her.

The call to circle the wagons was made, and she dreaded it. She waited until they were in their spot before jumping down. She almost tripped as she walked away from the wagon, but she quickly righted herself. She put down the tailgate and stared at the provisions, trying to figure out what kind of meal she could serve. Finally, she pulled out hardtack, dried beef, and a wheel of cheese. Then she brought out a crate and grabbed her shawl.

Essie would be fed first. Besides, if there was sickness she wanted Essie far away from other people. Essie latched on and began to nurse, but she seemed particularly hungry and feeding her was taking much longer than usual. When at last she finished, Cora buttoned up her dress and burped the baby. She reached into the wagon and took out Essie's basket. After kissing her dear girl, Cora placed her in the basket.

She got out the bag of buffalo chips she'd collected that morning and surprised herself by making a topnotch fire. She sure could use some coffee to stave off her weariness. After carefully roasting the beans in a pan, she let them cool then put them in the coffee mill. Soon she had the pot heating.

Harrison was taking longer than usual with the livestock. This day would never end. She dragged the tent out of the wagon herself and set it up herself. First she put Essie inside, and then she got her blankets. She didn't bother with a nightgown. She'd probably be woken up to cook soon anyway.

She'd barely gotten the quilt pulled up when she remembered her coffee, but upon hearing some grumbling from outside, she decided she'd do without. Straining, she thought she heard Heath and Declan talking about Zander. She couldn't hear the words but realized they weren't grumbling after all. Guilt and shame washed over her when she thought about the day. She'd embarrassed her husband and it wasn't right.

She threw the quilt off and put her shoes on. Then she lifted the tent flap and walked to the fire. With a glance, she noted that Harrison didn't have coffee either. After gathering two cups, she went to the fire and, using her apron she picked up the pot. She handed one of the filled cups to Harrison and poured one for herself. Afterwards, she lifted a crate and set it down next to her husband.

"I'm sorry I shamed you," she whispered. He didn't respond, making her feel even worse. She got up and made her bread dough for the morning. After cleaning up, she glanced at Harrison again but he continued staring into the fire. She didn't know what else to do. She lifted the flap, put her nightgown on, and went to bed.

"I'M SORRY I SHAMED YOU." The words echoed in his mind. He had hoped the accusations weren't true, but that sounded like an admission. Where had it all gone wrong? He'd thought they were on their way to building a life. He had thought they were a family. How long had she been meeting with Simps? The whole party saw her and Simps come out of the long grass together, all smiles. He must have picked those flowers for her.

Harrison threw his cup. He didn't play the fool well. He got up and checked on Zander. Declan was just getting ready to roll under the wagon. Heath had headed off to take first watch.

Harrison took his time banking the fire. He picked up his cup and put it in a crate with a few other dirty dishes. Drawing a deep breath, he went into the tent. Maybe he should have volunteered for the first guard duty, but leaving her alone would make the gossip even worse.

He undressed in the dark, and by the time he was finished, his eyes had adjusted. She looked so innocent lying there. So very, very young and naïve. Simps was a no good — But she didn't like Simps. She had made that plain earlier. In fact, she never talked to men except for his hired men and the captain.

He watched as her eyes opened and the sadness he saw in her gaze tore at him. He climbed under the blanket and pulled her into his arms. "Can you forgive me?"

Her eyes widened.

"I listened when I should have questioned. All week people have been hinting that something was going on between you and Simps. I ignored it until I saw you both come out of the grass last night. Then you two had conversations twice, though one sounded like a quarrel." He released a sigh and shook his head. "I'm a fool, Cora. You have proved repeatedly that you aren't devious or a cheater. I should have believed in the trust we share. I care for you, Cora. Can you forgive me?"

"I—I… No one has ever asked my forgiveness that I can remember. It's been one of the worst days of my life. I thought I lost my best friend and there was nothing I could do or say to make you believe me. Essie and I don't just need you, we enjoy being with you. We'd miss a part of our hearts if we didn't have you."

It was probably as close to an admission of love she could give right now. But it gave him hope. They'd been on the right road together, and vicious people had set out to ruin it.

"Are you crying?"

She nodded, the movement making her face brush against his chest. His union suit was getting wet, but he wouldn't pull away for anything. She fit perfectly in his embrace, and he'd never let her go.

"Is that your stomach growling?" he asked.

"I hardly ate all day, and I was sick."

"You're a lot thinner than when we left Independence."

"Yes, but I'm trim not thin. I can walk longer, work longer, and I'm stronger than ever. I think if I were too thin I wouldn't have enough milk for Essie."

"Make sure you eat. Put your portion aside before the others come to eat. They don't look like they'd eat as much as bears, but they sure can fill their bellies."

"I'm surprised my cooking hasn't been objected to. I haven't had a whole lot of practice. I never noticed before, but ever since I've had Essie I see to it I learn something new each day. I've been so blessed to have you and Essie." She was quiet for a moment.

He wondered if she had fallen to sleep, but her body felt tense in his arms, and her breathing hadn't evened out the way he'd grown used to.

She drew a ragged breath and released it. "I should tell

you when I was sick on the side of the trail people yelled… congratulations, and I didn't know why at first, but I figured it out." Another sigh came out. "Now I suppose people will ask who the father is."

"The father of a child that doesn't exist? This just gets crazier and crazier. I'll make sure everyone knows you weren't unfaithful." Inwardly he cursed himself. "I should have put a stop to it the instant I heard a rumor like that was going around. I didn't believe it, so I let it alone until Simps made fools of us both. I hardly know him."

"He's asked me to go walking with him a few times. He looked insulted when I said no. He must think I was a whore or *am* a whore…"

"I'll talk to Captain London in the morning." He rubbed her back until her even breathing told him she had fallen asleep. People didn't think their marriage was real. He'd have to remedy that somehow.

———

Captain London stopped at their fire the next morning. "We're going to push hard today. The group ahead of us has buried many in its party. I want to pass them and keep going so they don't try to join us. I can't take the chance of exposing any of you."

"Do you know what they died of?" Cora asked.

"My best guess is cholera. For some reason it strikes this area. That's why I've been making sure people drink good water. Some have been using water out of their barrels for washing up and soaking clothes. We'll have a meeting tonight after we circle. Make extra food this morning, we might not get much of a chance to stop."

He went to the next wagon to tell them the news.

"What should we do?" she asked Harrison.

"Keep away from anyone who has it. Be sure the water we drink is good water. I've heard of whole families being wiped out. I want you and Essie to ride with me today."

"What about Zander? Will he get it?"

"He should be fine." A pained look fell over his features. "Don't be surprised if people die rapidly. Some hang on before they die too, but they don't all die. Don't touch anything that doesn't belong to you, and if we pass other wagons stay as far away as possible from anyone on that train."

She nodded and then busied herself making extra biscuits, then corn bread, cooking plenty of bacon. She had a cobbler in the coals when the captain yelled "Wagons ho!"

She pulled it out and wrapped the Dutch oven in a blanket. Perhaps if it stayed warm, the dried apples would be soft enough to eat tonight. She put Essie in her basket next to Zander, and they were off.

She turned once they were on the trail. "Zander, were your bandages changed yesterday? I'm sorry I didn't get to them last night."

"Declan did it for me, ma'am. I do prefer you to Declan. He's not the gentlest person I know. I thought he would break the ribs that weren't broken." He shifted uncomfortably. "But I'm getting better. I was hoping to move to the other wagon next time we stop."

"You'd be more comfortable with your friends?"

He gave a nod.

She smiled at him and then turned, facing the front. A wagon was pulled to the side and a man was digging a grave. "How awful."

"The best we can do is pray for them," Harrison said.

"I've been so busy, I've lapsed in my nightly prayers. It's no excuse, though."

"Look, another wagon and another grave." Harrison said.

"It's a mother and baby. I wish we didn't have to see this." Tears came to her eyes. "What if something happens to Es—" Her throat closed and her voice stopped working.

"Put that thought out of your mind," he said gruffly. "Now we know why we need to keep going. The captain will keep us safe." He gave her hand a quick squeeze.

"I suppose I should tell you about Essie's father." When he didn't respond, she laced and unlaced her fingers to keep her hands busy. "When I was sold to the saloon, my job was to clean it in the mornings and do anything else that was needed, like the washing. The bartender kept me busy. Early every afternoon, a boy would come in and play the piano. He seemed shy, and it took about a year before he talked to me. We were fast friends after that, though. As we grew up, we took notice of each other in a different way. Four years after he first talked to me he proposed. I could hardly ever leave the saloon, but one day we got a chance. He told me what we —did… that it was all right since we were getting married. About a month after that I kept getting sick, and the madam demanded to know who I had been with. She told me I was pregnant. When I told her I was getting married, she laughed. I belonged to her, she said." Cora took a deep breath.

She risked a glance at Harrison from the corner of her eye, but he kept his eyes forward.

"Later that day, the bartender stabbed Rudy and—killed him. Then he told me we had an appointment early the next morning with a woman who would know how to get rid of my baby. One girl—her name was Macey—asked Eddie to get me out of town, and he did. I was grateful to him. He never touched me. He said maybe we'd get married in Oregon but I don't think he ever had any intention of marrying me. He got mad easily and I found it best to just agree with him and tell him I was sorry when I wasn't."

"Did you love Rudy?" He didn't even glance at her when he asked.

"I thought so. I thought myself to be very much in love with him. I'm sure we could have made a life. His parents would have had a fit though. But I know now he was more boy than man. And I also know that I didn't know what love was. I caused his death. I'm thankful for Essie, but I'm still mad that Rudy said it was fine for us to be together before we were married. It was a lie, but I guess since I lived in a whore house..." She shrugged. "I really don't know."

"Sometimes our desires take over our good sense. He sounds like a nice guy and he made a beautiful girl with you."

"I'll always be grateful. I missed him so. I thought of him all the time but since being married to you, I seem to think about him less and less. I think a part of me will always love him... in some way." She swallowed hard. It wasn't easy telling Harrison about her past.

"I found that to be the same with Ora. I used to think of her all the time. My heart was so empty and it pained me. Then after you and I married, I thought I'd betrayed her memory." He glanced at Cora. "I will always have love in my heart for her."

They rode by the wagon train. The people looked defeated. It was hard to lose a loved one.

A few hours later, another scout, Oscar Randolph, rode down the line giving each driver instructions. They would stop for the nooning after all. The party they had just passed was stopping for the day.

There were plenty of buffalo chips just off the side of the trail, and she put Essie in her sling and hurried off to collect them. Everyone stood quite a distance from each other. Harrison came to help her when he finished unhitching the oxen and moving Zander into the other wagon.

"This is a nice surprise."

"I want everyone to know that we are together and we care for each other." He bent and kissed her lightly on the lips.

A wide smile spread across her face. "I do believe we will be the topic of conversation while people eat."

"That's the plan, sweet." He took Essie from her and held her against his big shoulder and then held the bag for her to put the chips in.

"I was thinking about the people who started after us. Will there be enough chips for them?"

"Chips, probably. Grass and wood might get scarce. I heard groups that left late last year had to drive their livestock more than a few miles away from the camp to find grass. Two of the reasons I signed on to Captain London's company were because he has a great record and he was leaving early. We hit snow at the beginning but better than at the end."

A big gust of wind lifted the sand from the ground and made it impossible to see. She closed her eyes and hung onto Harrison. It was getting hard to stay upright.

"Hold on and follow me!" he yelled above the strong gusts. It was hard, sand was in her eyes, nose, and mouth, and she worried about Essie.

Once back to their wagon, Harrison put Essie in her basket and lifted Cora into the back. "Pull the front as tightly closed as you can!" He climbed in a minute later and cinched the canvas at the back closed. Everything was covered in a layer of dust, but the worst of it was now being kept out. They moved things around until they had space for both of them to sit. It was a tight fit, but they made do.

Cora wiped Essie off as best as she could and then fed her. While she did that, Harrison turned the basket upside down and got as much dust as he could out of it before Cora set Essie back in it.

The wagon swayed back and forth and Cora put her arm on her husband's arm.

"Scared?"

She nodded. "What's going on?"

"It's a dust storm, but I saw lightning a long ways away. We might be in for a rain storm too."

"We have food made all ready and the extra water jug is full."

The wind hit hard again, and the wagon shuddered. Puffs of dust got in around the cinched up canvas.

"Grab one end," Harrison said as he handed her a corner of the tent. "We'll cover all our belongings on my left side. We'll cover the rest with the extra canvas. I can definitely smell rain in the air."

They worked quickly and covered much of the wagon, leaving a space for them to climb under. Then Harrison checked outside and made sure the wagon was secured.

Then suddenly the air cooled and she shivered. Lightning lit up the whole wagon followed by a huge boom. She jumped. Then the sound of rain as it hit the canvas was harder than any rain she'd ever heard before. After grabbing all the blankets she put them in the middle of the wagon for them. The extra canvas could easily be pulled to cover them if needed.

The wagon swayed and tilted as if one wheel had been lifted off the ground. Before she knew it, she was on Harrison's lap with her face against his chest. His strong arms went around her.

She turned her head, seeking her baby and was amazed. Essie was sleeping away.

More lightning and then thunder that made the ground shake. It felt nice being so close to Harrison, but she was still frightened. The wind picked up again, and the rain seemed to be coming down sideways through the small opening left in the back.

Harrison eased her off his lap and told her to lie down. He pulled the extra canvas over them and wedged himself down between her and a trunk. Essie's basket was toward the front above Cora's head.

"This is cozy," he teased.

"I'd like to try cozy when—"

Lightning cracked as though it had struck close by. Rain poured and poured, and she couldn't help jumping at each sound. "What about the livestock?"

"Heath and Declan will take care of the animals. I wouldn't be surprised if they were out in this trying to calm the livestock. Too bad we didn't circle for the nooning, we could have put some livestock in the center of the circle."

It sounded like rocks were dropping out of the sky. She snuggled closer until there wasn't an inch between them. "Hail?"

"Sounds like it. I hope the canvas holds up. If it doesn't, you can fix it from the inside or I could take it down to be repaired. I still can't believe Eddie thought you should climb up and sew the hole in his canvas shut."

A weak laugh slipped out. "I was stupid enough to go along with him."

"Ah, sweet, you were doing what you could so you and Essie stayed safe. It must have been hard knowing he could make you leave anytime he wanted."

"It was, but by the grace of God I'm here with you." After another flash of lightning and rumble of thunder made her heart race, she said, "Tell me again what we will do in Oregon."

"We'll file a land claim. I can have more land now that I'm married. Then we'll build a small house to keep us warm in the winter and a barn. We'll buy a milch cow and enough food to get us through to spring." The deep calming tones of his voice settled her fears. She could listen to him talk like this forever and never feel pressed upon. "I'll buy more cattle and horses. I'll have to see how bad the winter is and if the livestock will need extra feed. Might as well grow what they eat. I'll till the earth for you to have a big garden. Then we'll sit outside and watch the sunset. Then of course a bigger house will be built as our family gets bigger."

"How much bigger?"

"As big as God blesses us."

She kissed his neck. "I like your plan. How much farther do we have to go?"

"Just another four months."

She laughed. "So a very long time."

"When I'm with you, time goes by quickly."

She giggled softly. "Harrison, you are such a charmer."

She felt him shift a bit and then his soft masculine lips were on hers. The love in his heart could be felt in his kiss. It was so beautiful, and she wanted the moment to last forever. They were so busy kissing they didn't notice that the storm had passed until they heard loud voices crying out. People must need help.

He kissed her one more time and eased the canvas back. "I need to get out there and see what I can do."

She smiled and nodded, unable to think of any words. He must have truly kissed her senseless.

CHAPTER EIGHT

One wagon had blown over, but everyone seemed to have made it through with only minor injuries. Most of the wagons were soaked. They probably didn't think to put the other canvas over their things.

"Zander, are you all right in there?" Harrison opened the cinched back of his second wagon.

"I'm fine. Heath and Declan were out in it though. Mrs. Chapman said I can get up and around in a few days. I'll be glad to be out of this wagon."

"I bet. Were you able to stay dry?" Harrison didn't see many puddles inside the wagon.

"I put our oil cloths over the important stuff and had the blankets over me. It must have been worse than I thought."

There was a lot of crying and wailing going on.

"Tell the other two to check in with me when they get back. I'll see what the wailing is about."

Harrison stopped by the Waverly's wagon. Their dry food was wet. Their flour and cornmeal were beyond saving. He checked in on the Chapmans. Mr. Chapman told him that the missus. was out playing doctor again. Next, he noted that

87

the overturned wagon belonged to Eddie. Harrison wanted to believe he got what he deserved, but the man did rescue Cora from the saloon.

He helped a weeping Emily Swatt hang her soaked blankets and clothes. She hadn't checked her food yet. He didn't warn her about what she might find; her husband would probably be back soon.

Sue Bandor was bandaging her husband Miller's head. He'd been out with the livestock.

He hoped the boys checked in soon.

Cora had built a fire and was making coffee and she had a big pot of water heating. He smiled. She must have dug a pit and made the fire in it. The ground was probably too soaked.

He got to the wagon the same time as Mrs. Chapman.

"Cora, thank you for heating the water. Do you mind if I bring the patients here to treat? It'll be much easier since the water is here."

Cora's face turned red. He walked to her and took her hand in his. "That would be fine, Mrs. Chapman."

As soon as Mrs. Chapman was out of hearing distance Cora frowned at him.

"Why are we having the very people who shunned me brought to our fire to use our water?"

"The right thing to do is to help those who need help. We came through the storm just fine with the grace of God, but most have soaked wagons. The Waverly's flour, corn meal and who know what else is wet, and it'll end up moldy and unusable. Eddie's wagon turned over. I wanted to say good and leave him to it, but then I remembered he rescued you from the saloon."

"You're right. I'll let the Waverlys know they can make bread and whatever else with their wet supplies. I think bread will last much longer than wet flour."

"Before you go, ask for some buffalo chips. I'll enlarge the pit you dug, and we can let many use the fire."

The smile he received had his heart flipping in his chest. She reminded him of a beautiful flower among weeds. Soon he'd ask her about a wedding night, but he'd have to ease into it. She didn't seem happy with that whole aspect of life. He picked up Essie and held her. Such a small baby, and he loved her as if she were his. He looked up to the heavens and smiled. No... not as if... She *was* his.

CORA STOPPED by wagons of the women who had at one time gossiped about her and offered them a place at her fire. All accepted, though a few had the grace to look embarrassed. They'd hurt her, true, but this was a second chance for friendship.

It was busy at the fire. The pit had been enlarged again, and there was now room for many to bring their tripods with pots to hang over the fire. Several of the women made bread with their wet ingredients and kept track of what they used so they could give dry flour back in return.

Heath and Declan straggled in.

"We held on to all of your livestock, Harrison," Declan said proudly.

"We sure did," added Heath. "I thought for sure we'd die out there, but we must be fine with the good Lord seeing as he didn't strike us with lightning." He laughed at his own joke.

"Sit, the both of you. Any injuries?"

"We must have hard heads," Declan said seriously.

"I brought Zander a plate," said Cora. "Let me fix plates for you." She went to the tailgate and put bread and corn bread and flapjacks on their plates. She handed the food to the two men. Then she stood straight up and put her hand over her heart and gasped.

She stepped away from the others and went to a lone man standing there with his horse. She must be seeing things. The closer she got she thought it unbelievable. Rudy was dead. She stopped in front of him and stared at him.

"But… you're dead. Bosley killed you."

"He stabbed me," said Rudy in a grim tone. "But I pulled through. I knew I had you and our baby out there, probably alone. It took me a long hard time, but I've found you." He embraced her.

Tears poured down her face. Rudy, her Rudy was alive. It was a miracle and he'd need to meet his daughter…

Her heart fluttered. She was married to Harrison now. Taking a step back, she broke the embrace. Harrison was watching her, and he looked concerned. She locked her gaze on him as he strode over.

"I haven't seen you before," he said with more than a hint of suspicion in his voice.

"I'm Rudy Downing. I'm a friend of Cora's."

"Nice to meet you, Rudy." His eyes flickered to Cora then settled back on Rudy. "I've heard a lot about you… mainly that you were dead."

"Yes, that's what Cora just said. And you are?"

"I'm Harrison Walsh. Cora's husband."

Rudy's eyes filled with confusion and then accusation as he turned to her. "People said the man didn't marry you. He was just taking you west with him."

She needed to sit down. "That was Eddie. He wasn't the nicest of men, and I had nowhere to go when he turned me out. Harrison married me and has been taking care of me and Essie."

A smile lit his face. "I have a daughter? Where is she?"

There wasn't a place to hide. Not a tree in sight. Everyone

was at her wagon. How many times had she cried for Rudy? And now he was here. He looked hurt, yet something else glittered in his eyes.

"Pack your things. We can start for home."

She shook her head. She stared at Rudy and then at Harrison. How could she leave the man she was falling in love with? But how could she keep Rudy from his child? It was a horrible decision, one she didn't want to make. She turned and ran. She kept running until she was too tired to run anymore and a river blocked her way. She sat and put her head against her knees and cried.

Oh Lord, what am I to do?

She heard the clip clop of the horse's hooves but she couldn't look up. She loved one with all her heart, yet the other had looked for her for months and he was Essie's father.

She still had her eyes closed, but she knew who it was. His scent was so familiar to her. He sat next to her and his arms went around her. He didn't say a word, just rocked her back and forth. She laid her head upon his shoulder and took in a deep shaky breath which she let out slowly.

"You must think me a child running like that. I just couldn't stand there while you both stared at me." A tremor rolled through her. "Harrison, I never thought to see him again. Dead is final. Back there… I thought I was seeing a ghost. I looked up and there he was. He's been looking for me for months. He thought me to be unmarried and traveling with Eddie. I feel so guilty, yet I don't see that I would do anything differently. There was so much blood…"

"I'd never thought of you as a child," he said gently. "You are a fine, caring, loving woman. You make my blood stir every time I look at you. I've never loved another the way I love you. I thought it an odd thing that my wife's name was Ora while yours is Cora. At first I thought of it as you being like her but having an extra letter in your name. Now I see Ora as missing a letter in hers." He shook his head. "I'm not making sense, am I? You've filled my heart like no other woman has ever filled it. You add the fun and goodness to my days. I love Essie, and I don't know if I could bear to have you both ripped away from me. I saw a flower surrounded by weeds and thought of you as the flower, the survivor that stood up taller than the weeds." He chuckled. "Plus you're beautiful. I know this is a lot and you have much to think on. I'll give you time to think. Spend time with him and make a choice. Because if—" His voice cracked, and he swallowed hard. "If you stay with me, I want you... all of you. For you to be my wife, for me to make a life beside you."

She put her arms around Harrison, gave him a hug and drew away so she could see his face. There were unshed tears in his eyes. "I do want to spend time with him, but only to make sure he understands that my life is with you. You have been my rock. I can depend on you to keep me and Essie safe. No one has ever made me feel more loved. You make me feel special and pretty even." A smile tugged her lips upward. "And don't forget we have a whole passel of children to raise."

"We'd have to make them first," he said, returning her smile.

"Where is Essie?"

"Zander has her, and Heath and Declan are guarding her. Apparently Zander and Essie became the best of friends when he traveled in our wagon. She is very taken with that Irishman. I will have to build a big house with locks on the bedroom doors to protect my daughters from men with the gift of gab."

Laughing, she was almost feeling herself again. "Did Rudy hold her?"

"No, sweet, I thought that was between you and Rudy.

Besides you should be the one to hand her to him to hold. Yes, a man should hold his daughter. He can't keep her, mind you, but he came all this way. I wonder what his parents had to say."

"I can only imagine." She reached up and touched his cheek. "You're a kind, giving man."

"Let's go back and see our daughter," he said before he kissed her.

He mounted up and reached for her, and when she reached back, he helped her up in front of him.

"Will the wagons make it across the river? It looks like mud with a bit of water covering it."

"This part of the Platte River is known for that. We'll take it slow and listen to what Captain London tells us to do."

"Sounds like we have more hours of travel. He'll want to circle up near the river, won't he?"

Harrison nodded his agreement. "He'll want to be first in line for a river crossing."

Cora sat back until she was leaning against her husband. She'd have a long talk with Rudy. Everything would turn out fine. It had to.

A RIDER on a dark bay headed toward them at a fast pace. The scout, Oscar Randolph reined in, his horse's hooves tossing up clods of dirt. "That man took your baby!"

"Hold on, what happened?" Harrison asked.

"The man who says he's Essie's pa took her."

"Which way did he go?"

"The way back east. Simps took off after him, but I thought I'd best get you."

Harrison felt Cora stiffen. A glance at her revealed she

had turned her lips inward, and she blinked as though fighting tears.

"I'll need to have a new mount. I'll stop long enough to grab one and go after our daughter." He urged his horse forward. "Yaw!"

Their mount lurched ahead, and they rode quickly. Harrison barely stopped the horse before he slid off and helped Cora down. He raced to their wagon and grabbed some supplies in case he was gone more than a day.

"Harrison, I'm going with you!"

"Cora, no, you'll slow me down."

"Harrison, Essie will need to be fed."

He stopped in mid-stride. "Fill a carpet bag with a few essentials and clothes for Essie. I'll meet you at the boys' wagon."

Heath and Declan had one horse saddled and ready. "I will need a second horse. A fast one. I don't think Cora knows how to ride. We'll double up and keep switching horses."

"We're sorry boss, we were guarding the back of the wagon and Zander fell asleep and that sneaky bandit just stole her," Declan explained.

Heath hurried toward them with a second horse just as Cora arrived. They tied the carpet bag and bed roll on the second horse.

Harrison practically threw her up on the horse and swung up behind her. He kicked the sides of the horse, and they were off in a thunder of hooves. He couldn't go as quickly as he wanted, not with two riders; it would tire the horse too quickly.

Rudy had the baby with him, which should slow him down. She was probably hungry, which meant she would be fussy. Determination to get the child back swelled within him. Rudy had a right to be angry and disappointed, but he had no right to kidnap Essie.

Cora appeared to be holding up better than many mothers would have. She'd had to be tough plenty of times in her life. He peered from side to side. There wasn't anything to hide behind in the sand pit they rode through.

A rider heading their way along the trail turned out to be Simps returning. He shook his head. "He's gone. Not a sign of him. And I can't leave the train. Captain London depends on me."

Cora stiffened, but Harrison nodded in agreement. "We have to keep going."

The other wagon train was still circled when they reached it, and Harrison stopped. An older woman with a faded yellow poke bonnet and a gray dress waved her arms trying to get his attention.

"Are ya looking for that man with the baby?"

"Yes."

"He's hidin' in the widow Plum's wagon. He's going to marry her. I think he just needs a mother for his girl."

Cora gasped. "She's *my* baby. He stole her."

"Best hurry, I know the preacher is getting ready to get them hitched."

"Where's the captain?"

A man walked over with a look of concern on his face. "I'm right here. Can I help you folks?"

"I'm here for my baby. She must be hungry by now."

"What's this?" His eyebrows rose. "That young fella with the baby girl? We'll need to get to the bottom of it before he marries the widow. Follow me."

They both dismounted and followed the captain. He wore a cap like a sea captain would wear. It would have been amusing if they hadn't been so on edge.

They could hear Essie crying before they saw her. Cora took off and ran to the wagon.

A woman in an expensive dress came out of the wagon holding Essie. "I'm afraid you're mistaken," she insisted. "This is my daughter. Who are you?"

"I'm Cora Walsh, and that is Essie Walsh, and right behind me is my husband Harrison Walsh. If she's yours, then you'll need to feed her. I last fed her over four hours ago."

The woman held Essie closer to her.

The captain walked until he was right in front of the widow. "Now, Uma, you know you don't have a baby. We just buried your husband three days ago."

"Cholera?" Harrison asked.

"Yes, we've had a bad outbreak of it." The captain looked inside the wagon. "Why don't you come on out of there and explain yourself."

Rudy climbed out of the wagon and glared at Harrison. "She's *my* daughter."

"No one said she wasn't. But you can't just up and steal a baby. How was she going to be fed? Did you bring diapers? Blankets? What exactly was your plan? From what I understand, you have folks in Independence. Are you leaving them behind?"

A sullen expression fell over Rudy's face. "I stopped here looking for Essie and met Uma. She'll make an excellent mother. Now I suggest you leave."

"I'm not leaving without my daughter," Cora said in a chilly voice. She approached him. "I thought you were dead." She poked him in the chest. "I never denied you are her father." She poked him again. "I was feeling bad for you since I married Harrison, but you kidnapped her." She poked him once more, and he winced.

Harrison put his arm around Cora's waist and steered her away from Rudy.

"Do your parents know where you are and what you are doing? Do you have money to start a farm or ranch in Oregon? I don't think you've thought this all out. We are standing in a camp where they've had cholera. You exposed yourself and Essie to it. Probably Harrison and me too. Rudy, you were my first love, but it was the love of a girl, not of a woman, and even though I know it wasn't your fault, you weren't there for me, for Essie and me. And now? It wouldn't work between us."

Rudy sighed and his shoulders sagged. "I didn't tell my parents I was going. They're probably worried. But I know they can provide a life for Essie. She's *my* daughter."

Cora walked up to the widow and held out her arms. The widow seemed reluctant, but after a deep sigh, she handed Essie to Cora.

"If you'll excuse me, I need to feed my daughter." Cora walked to where the horses had been left and grabbed a small blanket from the carpet bag. Then she sat down and fed Essie while covering herself with the blanket.

"We're taking Essie with us," Harrison said.

Rudy nodded his head. "It's… well, I had so many plans for the three of us. It never occurred to me that Cora could love another man. I suppose I should go back to my family. If I'm ever in Oregon, though, I'll expect to meet my daughter. For now I'm—I'm going home."

"Going home?" screeched the widow. "You proposed to me! What kind of man are you?"

"A desperate one." He untied the reins of his horse and mounted up. "Tell Cora and Essie I said goodbye. I can't—I just can't." He kicked the sides of his paint and off he rode.

Harrison joined Cora. "We need to wash off. I should have had you do it before you fed Essie." He took one canteen and a cloth. After wetting the cloth he washed his hands. Then he washed Essie and put clean clothes on her.

He handed the canteen to Cora. "Wash your hands, breasts and face. Once we get near our party, we'll have someone bring out some lye soap and clean clothes for us.

He looked up at the sky. "We should have just enough time to make it back before dark."

CORA COULDN'T HELP but fret over the possibility that they were exposed to cholera. That woman had held Essie close, even though her husband had died of it. What if Essie got sick or Harrison or herself? It should have been unthinkable, but it was all she could think of.

They neared their party, and Harrison told everyone to stand back. He asked Heath for any water that had been sitting so the sand was at the bottom along with lye soap and some towels.

Then he asked Sally Waverly to bring them all clean clothes to wear. Everyone was worried for them. All the men turned their backs to give her privacy of sorts. Harrison held up a blanket for her too. They had more than enough water, she even washed her hair. She set the clothes she wore in a pile. Next, she washed Essie and then her own hands again before they dressed. Harrison did the same. He also washed down the canteen, the saddles and then took everything out of the carpet bag and threw it in the pile.

"Heath, take the horses and wash them down by the river. Take soap with you." Harrison tossed the reins to him.

"Stand back. I need to burn the pile."

Cora's jaw dropped. Her clothes, the sling, her carpet bag. She watched as it all went up in smoke. Her heart pounded, sending blood rushing in her ears. They were just things, right? Better to lose them than to cause death by trying to keep them.

Harrison took her hand and led her to the wagons. "I think it best if no one comes close to us for a few days until we know if we're infected. Rudy hid in one of the wagons in the party we passed. They were hit pretty hard. I made sure we washed as soon as we left camp and just now we scrubbed ourselves. All we can do now is wait. We'll take the back of the line for the next few days and keep to ourselves."

Captain London came forward. "That's more than most folks would have done. I appreciate the steps you've taken to prevent illness. We will cross the South Platte in the morning. We managed to dry out a bit. Your fire is still going." He nodded to them and walked away.

"Do you think we'll get sick?" she asked Harrison.

"I will say a lot of prayers in the next few days." He took Essie from her arms and held the baby against his shoulder. With his other hand, he captured Cora's. "Here, sit down and get warm by the fire."

"Look, they left us plenty of pancakes and cornbread." Cora smiled.

"Good, now we won't have to fix anything," Harrison said. "It's almost dark."

"How does cholera start? A fever? Bad stomach? A cough?" She caught her bottom lip between her teeth. How long would they have to wait to be sure?

"Yoo-hoo!"

"Hello, Mrs. Chapman," Harrison greeted.

"I won't come any closer, but I want to tell you to be sure to drink plenty of good water. If you feel sick at all, keep drinking. It keeps fevers at bay if you can drink. I'll check on you from time to time. There isn't any medicine that treats cholera. Not everyone gets it, so don't panic."

"Thank you, Mrs. Chapman," Harrison replied. "We should eat and get enough rest. Keeping up our strength is important."

"I'm so sorry, Harrison. You wouldn't have been exposed if not for me." Cora leaned her elbow on her knee and rested her chin on her hand.

"We're in this together, sweet. We'll get through it. I know it." He grazed her cheek with his knuckles. "You're shaking."

"It's just hitting me I almost lost Essie. I had nice memories of Rudy, but not anymore. He kidnapped our baby, and I should have walloped him!"

"Walloped?" His chuckle filled the clearing. "To think I thought you as meek as a mouse." The laugh faded, and his expression grew somber. "I don't blame you for being upset. He betrayed your trust. Though he had a different picture of what would happen when you saw him. He expected to spend his life with you. That does not excuse what he did, but when your dreams are ripped away suddenly, it's painful. When Ora died, I thought I wanted to die with her. I sometimes have nightmares about the way she died. The agony she bore and her screams. Maybe if I was unselfish, I would have suggested you go with him but where you and Essie are concerned I'm very selfish. I have to admit it scared me when I realized who he was."

"Unsure of me?"

His headshake was quick, almost fierce. "Unsure of us both, and I shouldn't have been. If you *had* left... well I don't want to think about it again."

She stood and wrapped her arms around his waist and put her head on his chest. "Essie doesn't seem to mind sharing you."

He kissed the top of Cora's head. "No, she doesn't mind at all. I'm exhausted. Today took an emotional toll on us both. Why don't we eat and then get to bed? You don't mind if I cram into the wagon with you? It's dark, but I could put the tent up."

"No, the wagon will do nicely. My mind won't quiet. I keep thinking what if we hadn't found Essie?"

"We would have searched until we found her. I bet Zander feels bad about the whole thing."

"I bet all three of them do. When we get to Fort Laramie, will you write your mother about our marriage?" She wished she hadn't asked. His mother didn't sound like the nicest person.

"Of course, and I will also tell her I was twice blessed. I now have a wife and a daughter. She'll have something to say about it, but that's just how she is. She made Ora miserable and she knew it. I think people who aren't ever happy take it out on others. That was why we were so excited to leave for Oregon. Sometimes it seems like yesterday and other times it seems so long ago that it was a different life. Like now having both of you in my arms, I can't imagine my life without the two of you."

Warmth rushed through her. "You say the sweetest things."

CHAPTER NINE

"Gather round!" called Captain London. "We're crossing the Platte River today. I know you're tired, but we're crossing before a huge line of wagons appears. The water isn't deep, but as always, we need to have a care. Things can happen in a river. We'll drive the livestock across first. After we cross there's a hill we must climb, and then we will use ropes to lower the wagons. There is a foot-path for people to walk down. I'd rather not have anyone in the wagons while they are being let down. There have been accidents and wagons have crashed into pieces. I know I've been encouraging you all to lighten your loads. This would be one of the best times to do it. Harrison, you'll be at the end. Normally I'd appreciate your help but maybe you should sit this one out. Don't worry, we'll get your wagon down. After the crossing, send Cora and Essie up the hill and then down the path. I'm sorry but they must sit away and have their own fire."

Harrison nodded. "Understood."

"Folks, it will be worth it when you're down at Ash Hallow. You'll think you've found paradise. The water is clean, there is plenty of wood, and it's a real pleasing place." He gazed over the gathered crowd. "The first few wagons hurry and get packed up. This will be an all-day project."

Declan came close but not too close. "I'll be driving the cattle over. There are plenty of men willing to help with the livestock. I'll get them settled and come back to help lower the wagons."

"You're a good man, Declan," said Harrison.

Declan smiled as he turned away.

"Looks like we won't have to hurry getting packed up since we're last," Harrison commented as he made a fire. "We have time for coffee and breakfast."

"That would make you happy?"

"Yes it would, my enchanting wife." He loved when she blushed. He watched as she finished feeding Essie. His desire for her grew but was she interested in having a close relationship? Sometimes she seemed almost too innocent to have had a child. Liking his kisses had obviously surprised her, and he knew she thought about it often since she stared at his lips. Rudy wasn't any older than Cora; perhaps he had had no experience. For someone who lived among whores, she didn't know very much about desire or responses. If Ash hollow was as scenic as the captain said, it might be the perfect place to make their marriage real.

Cora handed him a cup of coffee. "You're deep in thought. They will help with our wagon, won't they?"

"I'm sure they will. I wish I could be of some use. The captain was right about wagons being destroyed. That's why I brought two wagons so I wouldn't have a heavy wagon. I've seen the furniture inside some wagons, and I hope they leave some of it behind."

She tilted her head to the right. "You're awfully knowledgeable about the trail."

"I rarely make fast decisions. When we first thought

about going west, I read everything I could get my hands on. I went into Independence and listened while captains and guides told their stories of the trail. They said it was hard, but they also made it a big adventure. It's certainly been both."

"You're not kidding, though I could do with a little less adventure. I'm so glad I met you and you were practically forced to marry me." She chuckled and leaned down, kissing his cheek.

He didn't move. It was the first time she'd kissed him. It felt so right, but he had to put it out of his mind. At least until they got to Ash Hallow.

"Look! Zander is walking!" she exclaimed.

Harrison turned his head and nodded in approval. "Can't keep him down for long. He's had a hard life. Most of his family starved during the Irish potato famine. He almost died on the ship coming to America, and he was penniless when he arrived. I'm not sure what he did for his first year but he met up with Heath and Declan and they decided to go west and get some free land."

"That must have been horrible to watch loved ones die of hunger. I never heard much about it. He's found a new family with Heath and Declan, and I hope they consider us family too. Plus he's young and handsome, and I doubt he'll have trouble finding a wife."

Harrison opened his mouth in mock outrage. "Been looking at the single men, have you?"

She turned crimson. "I did have to help take care of him. I doubt it would have worked if I closed my eyes. The bandages might have ended up everywhere except where they were needed." She sat on a crate and sighed happily. "Being with you is so different from being with Eddie. There was never laughter allowed, and it always filled me with fear."

"He still watches you, so be careful around him. I think he believes you belong to him."

"Well I don't, and he needs to remember that." She shuddered. "He went through with his threat of leaving me with nothing, and it was the best thing that ever happened to both me and Essie."

She watched some of the wagons line up. "Do you think the boys will have land near us? That would be nice, wouldn't it?"

Essie began to fuss, and Harrison picked her up and rocked her. "You have months to win them over to your ideas. It would be nice though. They'll marry someday and Essie will have little ones to play with."

The baby reached up and touched his nose. She took her hand away. Then she reached up again and wrapped her fingers tight around it. He carefully pried one finger at a time off his nose and stared at the baby. "She's got a strong grip."

"Wait until she grabs your hair, you'll wish you didn't have any."

"To think how boring my life would be now without the two of you. Both sweet except one can be painful. Do you think she'll start pulling my ears?"

Cora put her hand over her mouth as she laughed. "Now is that nice?" She laughed harder.

"I'm not sure you'll soon have anything to laugh about," Eddie said as he glared at them from a safe distance. "They say that the man you gave yourself to is dead. The same will happen to you."

"Don't get too close. I might be tempted to choke you and then you'll become infected. Your best bet is to keep your mouth closed."

Eddie glared at them. "Someday Harrison won't be here to protect you." He strode back to his wagon, climbed up and drove his oxen to the end of the line.

"I don't even know if he's telling the truth. Do you think Rudy is dead?" she asked.

"How would he even know?"

She nodded.

There were still a few who weren't packed up.

"Relax, sweet, the line isn't moving any too fast. It'll be hours before we'll have our turn."

"That long to cross?"

"As soon as they're across they make the climb up the hill. It isn't a long trail just steep so the wagons get backed up. Some are waiting on the hill to be lowered and some are waiting for room to cross over. I've heard of large parties taking days to get over."

"I might as well cook extra food. I have a feeling we won't have much time to cook after we're lowered down."

He nodded. "You'll be exhausted. Any chance you can make some gingerbread?"

She nodded and smiled. "For you, anything."

HARRISON WAITED until there were only three wagons left in line before he pulled out from their spot and joined the wagons. He hated sitting idle when they could use his help. He understood the reasoning, it just made him restless. When he saw it was Tom Simps in charge of the river crossing, he wanted to groan but he kept silent. Cora didn't need the extra worry.

It was well past noon and they had been in line for a good hour. Finally, they were next to go across and Tom gestured for Harrison to drive his team into the water. Harrison shook his head no.

"I'm in charge here, and you do as I say," Simps warned.

"If I go now, I'd have to sit my wagon and oxen in the

river. There isn't room for me to pull up onto the opposite bank. I'm no greenhorn, Simps."

"I said go!" He slapped the back one of the front oxen causing a slight lurch forward.

But Harrison had a good hold of the lines. "You want us stuck to the bottom, isn't that right?"

"I have no idea what you're talking about."

Rod Waverly jumped down from his wagon on the opposite side and walked to the bank. "What are you trying to pull Simps? You know the bottom is like quicksand if you stop. The Walsh's seem to have enough problems without you trying to sabotage them. I thought one of your jobs as a guide was to get us where we're going," he yelled.

"Why can't people mind their own business? I'm in charge here," Simps insisted.

Chuck Swatt joined Rod. "Why would he want them to be in the river while they wait to cross? If those oxen get stuck, the whole wagon could tip. I will get the captain. I doubt he'll be happy to have to come back down the hill and then have to go back up again."

All three men stared at Simps until he finally walked away.

"Thanks for your support, Rod and Chuck. I appreciate the help!"

"Didn't look like you were planning to cross, but when he slapped the oxen, that was a line he shouldn't have crossed. He knows better than most what could happen," Rod yelled.

At last there was room on the other side of the river, and Harrison took his wagon into the water. The going tricky, but he accomplished it without incident. Cora had sat beside him, Essie in her arms. He breathed gusty sigh, relieved when they were across.

Once at the top of the hill, Harrison was shocked by the

drop. He hoped the ropes they used to lower the wagon weren't weakened by the other wagons.

"Harrison you might as well go down the footpath with your family. There will be plenty of other drop offs where you can help lower the wagons," Captain London told him from a distance.

Harrison gave him a quick nod. He smiled down at Cora, who looked relieved he would walk her down. He took the bag she carried.

"I can carry our daughter if you like," he offered

Cora's smile almost stopped his heart. It was filled with sunshine and love; more love than he'd ever felt before. He swallowed hard. Was he deserving of a love so powerful?

"I'll let you know after we start. The way the path goes one way and then the other way looks to make it safe enough."

The path wasn't wide, and they snaked their way down without incident. He tried not to look at the wagon being lowered. It was a miracle any of them made it. The wagon hit the ground hard, but it still looked fine. Next was their wagon and he held his breath and forgot to keep walking.

"Harrison?"

"I'm coming." He walked but couldn't keep his eyes off his wagon. It was less than a foot off the ground when one rope broke. It ended up being fine, but what if it hadn't been?

Thank you, God!

"That was close," Cora said breathlessly. They finally reached the bottom and she ran to the wagon with him not far behind.

He examined the wheels and axels. He then hitched up his oxen and led them to a quiet place a little away from the others.

Declan came along, unyoked the oxen and prepared to

lead them off. "We've eaten, but I gathered wood for you. I'll have Heath bring it."

"Thank you."

Heath came with an armful of wood while Declan left with the livestock. "Do you need anything else?"

"No, thank you. Where are you off to?"

"The water here is uncommonly clear. We're going swimming." He hurried off.

Cora laughed. "He probably thought you'd stop him if he stayed."

"I bet you're right. Let's get the fire going. I could use a hot cup of coffee."

"You make the fire, and I'll get the coffee ready. I roasted the beans already. Only enough for tonight. The coffee is better when fresh roasted." She placed Essie in her basket and ground the beans and had the coffee ready to go on the grate she set on the fire.

She turned in a big circle and her eyes sparkled. "Trees, water, and flowers; so much beauty after all that sand. It is beautiful."

He stared at her. "I agree with beautiful."

She blushed and ducked her head. He put his hands on her shoulders and waited for her to look at him. "I want to make this marriage real."

Her eyes widened and she turned her face away. He dropped his hands and grabbed two crates out of the wagon for them to sit on. He didn't know what else to say, so he said nothing.

She took out two cups and poured coffee for them both. She sat on her crate and stared into the fire. "I'm not a virgin," she whispered.

It took everything inside him not to smile. "That doesn't matter."

"I lived in a whore house, but I don't…" She turned her head away again.

"It was just Rudy," he whispered.

She nodded and turned back to him. There were tears forming in her eyes. "I've heard of women who hated that part of marriage, and I'm one of them. It terrifies me to think you'd want to do… that… every night. I don't know if I could stand it."

"Who told you that?"

"I hated it with Rudy and I heard the women talking about why men came to the saloon to see them. It was something wives didn't like to do." Tears rolled down her cheeks. "I've cheated you. You thought since I lived in one I was one or maybe not one but knew how."

He moved his crate closer to hers, reached out and plucked her from her crate before putting her down on his lap. He put his arms around her and rocked her back and forth. "I won't ask you to do anything you don't want to do. I won't have you live in fear that some night I'll hurt you."

"Why do you suppose some women like it and others don't? Rudy told me it would be the best moment of my life, but it hurt and left me bruised. I guess married couples do it to have children." She sighed and laid her head on his shoulder.

"It has to do with the man. If he's gentle and loving, women are fine with it."

She lifted her head and stared into his eyes. "Did Ora only do it to have a baby?"

He smiled. "A baby would have been real nice, but it expressed our love for each other. I believe she found it to be pleasing."

Her brow furrowed. "I'll have to think on this whole thing."

"Sweet, I already told you it was your choice."

"But would you go to a saloon seeking a woman?" She bit the bottom of her lip so hard it bled.

He wiped the blood away with his thumb before he kissed her gently. "I spoke vows when we were married, and I'd never do that to you. I love you."

Cora wrapped her arms around his neck and buried her face there. He rocked her back and forth until he felt her body relax. "Are you hungry?"

She jumped up. "I never offered you any food!"

He grabbed her hand and pulled her back onto his lap. "I'm not that hungry, I just wanted to be sure you weren't. To tell you the truth, I'm tired."

"We might as well sleep in the wagon tonight," she suggested.

"In a few minutes. I enjoy holding you."

Cora sighed contently. "I love you too."

CHAPTER TEN

*T*he next day Declan hauled water for Cora so she could wash clothes. Their time to use the spring was during supper time so they didn't come into contact with anyone. She couldn't wait to be wholly clean. She washed daily but to be in the water would be a great treat.

She watched the other women when they were with their husbands, looking for clues of affection. Sue Bandor was running around the fire while her husband Miller chased her. There was great laughter until he caught her. He scooped her up and kissed her soundly. They gave each other a look she'd never seen before. It was as though there was a secret they shared.

Sally shocked Cora by allowing her husband, Rod to steal a kiss while they hung the wet clothes on the line. Both couples seemed to have a closeness she'd never experienced with Harrison. It was all so confusing. She kicked at the dirt while she thought and noticed a stone-like object. She picked it up and wondered at its sharp point. She dropped it in her apron pocket.

So far, no one had been sick and she was so grateful. The

minister had prayed with them that morning, from a distance of course. They'd be just fine, she just knew it.

Harrison was making repairs to the wheels. It kept him busy, and that was a relief. She didn't know what to say to him. He hadn't asked her to decide about their marriage. Other women did their duty. Nothing made sense, and the more she thought about it the more frightened she became. Harrison said he'd honor his vows, but she'd heard too many men going up the stairs in the saloon. He'd want more children, a child of his own, surely. She enjoyed being a mother.

What was wrong with her? She tried it once and she didn't take to it. She wasn't a good wife. She was bound up so tight with her thoughts she wanted to cut loose and run. Instead she climbed into the back of the wagon and cried against the corner of the straw tick. She tried to be silent so Harrison didn't hear her and so she didn't wake Essie up. Finally she was cried out and she lay on her back staring at the canvas.

Harrison climbed in and kissed her forehead. "It'll all work out. I think one day it will just come naturally. I have no worries about it. We love each other, and that matters the most." He stretched out and pulled her into his arms. "It feels strange to be able to have extra time. Not that I mind."

"I thank God every day for you." She tilted her head until she kissed his jaw. "Close." She giggled.

"You sound like a school girl with that laugh."

"I'm just not old like you."

He laughed, and Essie wailed.

AFTER ESSIE WAS FED and changed, Cora gathered everything she'd need for taking a bath in the spring. Harrison carried Essie's basket while she carried a gunny sack. People smiled at them as they walked to the springs.

"It's lovely, Harrison. Too bad we can't just build a cabin here and live."

"That'd be something with all the wagons passing by," he teased. "Go on and get in I'll turn my back."

She peered around, making sure no one else was looking, and then quickly removed her dress. She left her chemise and pantalets on. Then she walked into the water and smiled at the heavenly coolness. "It's incredible."

He turned and started taking off his shirt.

"What are you doing?"

"Getting washed. Don't worry you can keep your back turned."

She did just that until she realized the soap was on the bank. She tried to get it while keeping her back to him, and he laughed so hard. The next thing she knew he picked her up in the water and threw her. Sputtering, she stood up and put her hands on his shoulders, trying to push him down in the water, but he was too strong. Shaking her head, she turned her back to him again and grabbed the soap.

"You aren't looking at me, are you?"

"Why would you think that?"

"I don't know why exactly, but I think you are." She scrubbed herself and her underthings with the soap.

"I think the only way to find out would be for you to look and see."

"You're smiling."

"How do you know?"

"I can hear it in your voice. I'm going to reach back and hand you the soap then I'm getting out. Even though I have clothes on, I don't want you peeking."

"If that's what you want." He took the soap from her.

She climbed out and smiled at Essie who was waving her hands in the air. Then Cora put on the dress she'd brought. She turned and was surprised to see Harrison's back to her.

There was something wrong with her. She felt disappointed. "I'll meet you back at the wagon."

"I'll be right there."

———

HE WAITED for a good minute before he turned around. Being a man of integrity had its drawbacks. He chuckled, remembering her face after he threw her. She probably wasn't allowed to have fun as a kid. Once they were settled on their land, he'd make sure she knew what it was like to have fun. His heart was so full of her. He drew a deep breath and stepped out of the spring. He looked around. He had a feeling he was being watched, but he didn't see anyone. He put his clothes on over his union suit and walked back to the wagon.

Cora was sitting all prim and proper next to the fire, drying her hair. She probably never thought of herself as prim and proper, but that was the only description that sprang to his mind upon seeing her. He watched her for a moment as she drew a comb through her long strands. Her hair sure was beautiful. He walked behind her and bent over, whispering in her ear, "I love you."

She ducked her head but not before he saw a smile. They'd be just fine. It would happen when they weren't thinking about it.

He dressed in clean clothes and climbed back out of the wagon. "I'm going to put the tent up."

"Harrison, do you know what this is? I'm assuming another settler dropped it but I don't know what it is." She handed her find to him.

"It's an arrowhead."

"From an arrow? An Indian arrow?" Her eyes filled with fright.

"I believe so." He glanced about. "I believe I need to go talk to the captain."

"I'm going into the wagon with our daughter and I will get the gun. Call out before you try to come in. I don't want to shoot you."

"I'll do that. I'll be right back." Perhaps someone *had* been watching him. He grabbed his rifle and searched for Captain London. He was with another family sharing coffee around a fire. Everyone turned as they saw him and the fear on their faces brought Harrison to a halt.

"Captain, I need to show you something, and frankly if we're not sick by now I doubt we will be."

Captain London nodded. "I was thinking the same thing." He stood and came to where Harrison stood. He then studied the object.

"Where was this and was it buried?"

"Cora found it. I doubt it was buried. It looks almost new to me."

"I think you're right. There's been sightings of Sioux in this area. Used to be one of the places they camped before the wagons started coming through. Though I didn't hear tell of any attacks. I'll double up the guards and you'd better move your wagon to our circle. I'll let everyone know you're not contagious any longer."

"Thank you. It'll make Cora feel safer."

The captain nodded and strode off, probably to set up the guard duty schedule.

Declan and Heath were by Harrison's side before he yoked the oxen.

"Did you see one?" Heath wanted to know. He took over hitching the oxen.

"No, just found an arrowhead, but I had a feeling someone was watching me while I was washing at the spring."

"We'll be extra vigilant. Captain London has enlisted us for guard duty. Zander will sleep in the wagon. The captain also said we're pulling out in the morning. No extra day," Heath told him.

"The best decision as far as I'm concerned. Some of the others are probably disappointed."

"You mention the word Indian and that disappointment goes away real fast," Declan said.

"I'm staying in our wagon with Cora and Essie. Be careful out there. Between the trees and the cliffs there are plenty of hiding places."

"We will," Heath said. They left, and Harrison shook his head. They almost seemed excited at the prospect of meeting up with an Indian. They did not understand what could happen.

"Cora, it's me." He climbed onto the front bench.

"What's going on?"

"We're joining the circle. The captain gave his approval."

"Thank the Lord! I've been sitting here praying."

"Your prayers must have been heard." He turned the oxen and found a space in the circle. What a relief. Hopefully they'll be safe. "I need to let the oxen free."

"I've got them," Declan said.

"Thank you." Harrison climbed into the back of the wagon. Cora was feeding the baby and for once she wasn't completely covered. It was beautiful, and not because he saw a bit more of her than usual. It was because a mother could feed her child from her own body. It was a revered moment for him.

Cora didn't even look up. Her face glowed as she gazed upon Essie. He expected her to blush, but she didn't. After she finished, she quickly covered back up and burped Essie.

It was a big step in their relationship. She didn't turn from him but allowed him to be part of it. How'd he get so lucky to have her in his life? It was now dark out, and he lit the lantern. They arranged the wagon so the straw tick lay nice and flat. Essie was fast asleep in her basket.

He lay on the mattress feeling content with his life. When Ora had died, he never thought to find peace again, let alone happiness. But a man never knew what path God would lead him to, and it was the best decision he'd ever made to listen with his heart.

Cora lay next to him and he enfolded her in his arms. "I love you so much, Cora."

"And I you."

He stilled. He'd been hoping and praying for her love. Finally she'd said it with conviction, like she really meant it. His heart filled and he never thought to feel so happy. He'd made his peace with Ora in the last weeks and any guilt he'd felt had gone away.

He began to think about the house they'd have and suddenly it occurred to him he might have to make it bigger. There were still several more months of traveling. They just might make a baby together in that time.

He'd resented having to marry but now he knew it was a gift. God never explained, he just did. As busy as Harrison was now, he'd be even busier once they got to Oregon. Enjoying time with Cora while they traveled wouldn't be hard to do.

He could hear his heart beat and it beat for Cora and Essie. He must have done something extraordinary to deserve both of them.

Thank you, Lord for Cora and Essie. Please keep us safe through our journey. My heart healed and now is overflowing. Ora used to be the one who talked to you instead of me. Now I realize there was a flaw in my thinking. We all need you in our lives. We need you to be part of us. I'm making a muddle out of this. What I mean is we aren't totally separate. I always thought of you as being a bystander watching but you are much more than that. You are part of every smile and kindness. I see you when I gaze at the land we travel. You are within me making me want to be a better man; a man of goodness, loyalty and high morals. A man who is willing to ask for your guidance. I think I'm on the right track and I praise you.

Cora stirred. "Not sleeping?"

"I'm dreaming while I'm awake."

"What?" her voice was drowsy.

"I'm thinking about the morning and all the mornings to come with you by my side. It's the best dream I've ever had."

"It's not a dream, Harrison, it's our future. Our very great and loving future. As soon as we can get a bit of privacy, I think I'd like to see for myself if you're right about marriage."

He chuckled and held her tighter. "Anything you say my love. I was thinking that maybe we could read the bible together. I'd like to get to know God better. I pray to him and ask for things but I never took the time to try to know him."

She was quiet for a while and he wondered if he said something wrong.

"I think it to be a wonderful idea. I know the basics but I've never had a bible to read before. I do know where we can get one."

Cora smiled and snuggled close to Harrison. Reading the bible was a wonderful idea. She'd always known God was with her. Harrison could help her if she didn't understand something and she could do the same for him. There were still many months to go and only God knew what the future of their journey would bring.

THANK you for reading Cora and Harrison's story. Book Two in this new series Romance on the Oregon Trail will pick up right where this one left off. Cora, Harrison and Essie will continue on while Declan has a heck of a time while he takes a wife.

Coming Soon- Luella's Longing (working title). Luella has a bad accident and recovers in Declan's wagon.

THE END

I'm so pleased you chose to read Cora's Courage, and it's my sincere hope that you enjoyed the story. I would appreciate if you'd consider posting a review. This can help an author tremendously in obtaining a readership. My many thanks. ~ Kathleen

ABOUT THE AUTHOR

Sexy Cowboys and the Women Who Love Them...
Finalist in the 2012 and 2015 RONE Awards.
Top Pick, Five Star Series from the Romance Review.
Kathleen Ball writes contemporary and historical western
romance with great emotion and
memorable characters. Her books are award winners and
have appeared on best sellers lists including: Amazon's Best
Seller's List, All Romance Ebooks, Bookstrand, Desert
Breeze Publishing and Secret Cravings Publishing Best
Sellers list. She is the recipient of eight Editor's Choice
Awards, and The Readers' Choice Award for Ryelee's
Cowboy.
Winner of the Lear diamond award Best Historical Novel-
Cinders' Bride
There's something about a cowboy

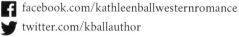

facebook.com/kathleenballwesternromance
twitter.com/kballauthor
instagram.com/author_kathleenball

OTHER BOOKS BY KATHLEEN

Lasso Spring Series

Callie's Heart

Lone Star Joy

Stetson's Storm

Dawson Ranch Series

Texas Haven

Ryelee's Cowboy

Cowboy Season Series

Summer's Desire

Autumn's Hope

Winter's Embrace

Spring's Delight

Mail Order Brides of Texas

Cinder's Bride

Keegan's Bride

Shane's Bride

Tramp's Bride

Poor Boy's Christmas

Oregon Trail Dreamin'

We've Only Just Begun

A Lifetime to Share

A Love Worth Searching For

So Many Roads to Choose

The Settlers

Greg

Juan

Scarlett

Mail Order Brides of Spring Water

Tattered Hearts

Shattered Trust

Glory's Groom

Battered Soul

Romance on the Oregon Trail

Cora's Courage

Luella's Longing

Dawn's Destiny

Terra's Trial

Candle Glow and Mistletoe

The Kabvanagh Brothers

Teagan: Cowboy Strong

Quinn: Cowboy Risk

Brogan: Cowboy Pride

Sullivan: Cowboy Protector

Donnell: Cowboy Scrutiny

Murphy: Cowboy Deceived

Fitzpatrick: Cowboy Reluctant

Angus: Cowboy Bewildered

The Greatest Gift

Love So Deep

Luke's Fate

Whispered Love

Love Before Midnight

I'm Forever Yours

Finn's Fortune

Glory's Groom

Made in the USA
Monee, IL
28 September 2021